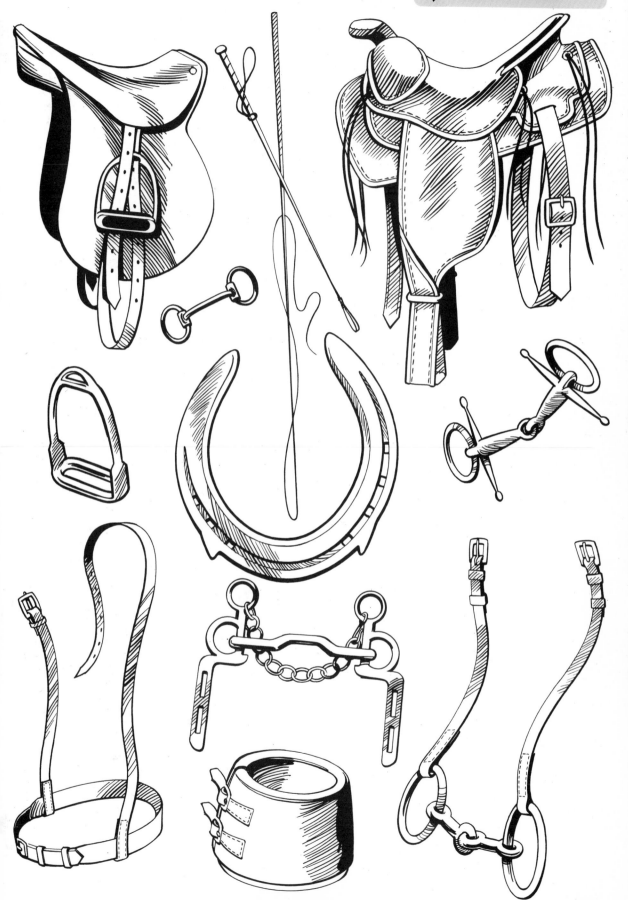

The illustrations in this book are by the following artists: *Mike Codd:* The Horse That Wanted to Change, Good-bye Bess, The Winged Horse of the Sky; *John Gillot:* The Saving of the Speed Herd, The Cross-Country Run, A Night Out, The Wild One, Two of a Kind, A Drastic Remedy; *Gary Rees:* Grani – the Pony of the Norsemen, Moon Maiden – a Pony in a Million, William and Mary, Little Mohee, Brunehilde – The Hanoverian, The Grey Mare is the Better Horse! *Peter Wilks:* Tony – The Movie Star.

Published 1979 by Purnell Books
Berkshire House, Queen Street, Maidenhead, Berkshire
Designed and produced for Purnell Books by
Intercontinental Book Productions
Copyright © 1979 Intercontinental Book Productions

SBN 361 04410 0

Printed by Purnell & Sons, Paulton (Bristol) and London

PURNELL'S TREASURY OF

HORSE
and
PONY
stories

**Written by Dorothy Baldock
Primrose Cummings
and Sally Haylor**

PURNELL

Contents

The Grey Mare is the Better Horse!

STANDING BY the steps of the stately white house that was the heart of the Sierra Estancia, Juan Gardenas looked up angrily at his father.

"Why should I ride Rosita?" he demanded petulantly. "She is old and slow and stupid!"

"She is nothing of the kind." Senor Roberto Gardenas returned his look calmly. "And you will ride her, my son, because I say so, and because I forbid you to take out El Diablo. Both of you are too young and too inexperienced to go out on your own or to do the work of a *gaucho* as yet. El Diablo will learn his trade from Manuel and you will learn yours from Rosita. Then, and only then, will I permit you and him to work the cattle together – no, Juan, not another word . . . " Senor Gardenas raised his voice, seeing his son was about to interrupt him, "Manuel, bring Rosita out, please."

From the nearby thatched stable came an old Mexican, his legs slightly bowed from years of riding. He was followed by a dusty-grey mare. She was tall and rangy and carried a Mexican saddle of faded scarlet leather, its high pommel shiny with wear. Ambling

7

over to the horse-rail the mare waited there, as she had done hundreds of times before, her head drooping patiently and her eyes half-shut against the bright morning sun. Juan looked at her contemptuously. What a poor creature she was compared with his black and beautiful colt, El Diablo!

"Mount up, Juan," said Senor Gardenas.

"Papa, please let me ride El Diablo." Juan turned to his father, making one last attempt to persuade him. "I ride him well enough and I know the *estancia* as well as you. Why can't I train him to be a true cattle horse? Let Manuel come with me on that old mare, if he must, or . . . or you – why don't you come with me instead?"

Senor Gardenas's heavy brows drew together, but before he could say anything, from the paved verandah, a girl's voice said quietly, "Juan, you're only making yourself look stupid and wasting everyone's time arguing like this. Rosita will teach you everything you need to know. *I* know – because she also taught me."

"You would say that, Dolores. You're only a girl!" Juan made a face at his sister. Used to her brother's remarks, she just shrugged good-humouredly and went on watering the baskets of brightly-coloured roses and carnations that edged the verandah.

"If you say so, *little* brother," she retorted. "But, if I were you I'd mount up, as Papa says, because if you wait much longer the sun'll

be hot enough to give you a heat-stroke, and as I've come home to have a holiday from nursing for two weeks, I don't want to have to spend it nursing you."

Juan knew he was defeated. He straightened the blue striped *zapara* that hung like a cape over his shoulders, and climbed, rather sulkily, into the saddle. El Diablo would have pranced excitedly now, tossing his head, but Rosita simply heaved a bored-sounding sigh and flicked her ears as her rider hooked his plaited leather whip over the pommel and gathered up the reins.

Senor Gardenas laid his hand on Rosita's neck. "Pedro is expecting you in Pampero Valley in one hour," he said. Then, ignoring Juan's mutter that El Diablo would have got him there in half that time, he went on " . . . you will take your place with the rest of the *gauchos* and help to drive the cattle to the valley head, cutting out the young bulls and heifers. Now, be off with you."

Had he been riding El Diablo, Juan knew he would have been able to swing the black colt dramatically round on his haunches and thunder away at a gallop, raising a cloud of red dust in his wake. Not so with Rosita. She turned slowly and deliberately and set off at a long striding trot that raised no dust at all.

Senor Gardenas watched his son ride down the long sycamore-shaded avenue.

"Perhaps I should have let you go with him, Manuel," he said. "Or have gone with him myself – then he could have ridden that colt of his."

But Manuel, pushing back his dusty felt *sombrero*, shook his head. "Indeed no, *senor*. He will learn more in one day from Rosita about the skills of a *gaucho* and the mysterious ways of cattle than he could learn from us in a week."

Senor Gardenas laughed at that. "You're right, and I am a fool to want to spoil my young son so."

"Indeed you are, Papa," said Dolores briskly. "Now, as I've finished watering the plants shall I pour you and Manuel some coffee, or would you prefer a glass of *tequila*?"

At the end of the avenue, by the little shrine to the Virgin Mary that his mother always kept decorated with flowers, Juan turned right on to a broad dust track. On either side were the *potreros* – the cattle paddocks fenced with barbed wire, where the calves grazed. But they were not grazing now, they were jostling each other at the fences, eager to watch Juan pass. There too, staring at him boldly, was a flock of black birds – the *tordos* – who always lived near the cattle.

"Good day, Senor Juan." Juan saw coming down the track towards him, an elderly woman with a dark *rebozo* covering her hair mounted on a sturdy *burro*. She drew her mount to a halt beside Rosita.

"So you're off to learn to be a *gaucho*," she went on. "My grandson, Pedro, will teach you well – he's not your father's finest cattleman for nothing. And you'll be a good pupil, mark my words; but where is your fine black colt?"

Juan stiffened. "I'm resting him today, Mama Michaela," he told her carefully. "That's why I'm riding this mare."

Mama Michaela, who seemed to know about everything that went on at the *estancia*, looked up at Juan with shrewd dark eyes. "And an excellent thing too," she said, adding with a chuckle, "never forget, Senor Juan, that sometimes the grey mare can be the better horse." And with that she clicked her tongue at the *burro* and trotted briskly on, leaving Juan staring irritably after her. What could she have meant? Rosita a better horse than El Diablo? How could she possibly be – Mama Michaela was just being foolish.

The paddocks ended and the grasslands – *campos geraes*, as Juan's Brazilian cousin called them – stretched before him like a rippling

green ocean, right up, it seemed, to the distant hills and beyond. Juan drew rein. He loved the scene; its vastness made him feel as if he was the only person in the world – a *gaucho* on a magic horse who could gallop faster than the wind. Then he remembered – he wasn't riding a magic horse, only Rosita.

"Well, old mare," he said, "let's see if you can gallop." He slapped the reins against her neck, and spurred her flanks.

Rosita snorted and broke into a canter. Then she extended herself into a gallop that, for a moment, quite startled Juan with its power and speed. But the moment didn't last, Rosita soon slowed down to the comfortable, steady canter again and nothing Juan could do would urge her out of it. He shouted, used his whip, spurs and *sombrero*, but Rosita would have none of it. She merely laid back her ears, and threw him a swift look over her shoulder that clearly said, "You can fuss all you like, I am *not* going any faster when there is no need to – and that is that!"

"Stupid creature," Juan muttered, admitting defeat for the second time that morning. And Rosita, realizing that she had won, settled into her favourite pace, a long striding canter, so effortless and rhythmic, that it seemed to eat up the grassland and almost lulled Juan into a doze. He still held the reins, but the mare needed.

no orders from him – she knew exactly what she was doing, and where she was going.

Gradually the flatness changed into a faint, but growing slope, and then rocks and clumps of grey-green cacti took the place of the grass. Dropping down to a walk, Rosita swung to the left, to pick up a rough uneven path that led through a strange cleft in the hills to Pampero Valley. Senor Gardenas had once told his son that the cleft had been formed by an earthquake many thousands of years ago. Juan preferred the Indian legend he'd learned from Mama Michaela, that the cleft was the result of a battle between two giants, who had torn up great handfuls of rocks to hurl at each other. He remembered that old legend now as the hills towered above him.

"It must have been quite a fight," he thought to himself and was so engrossed in living the story in his imagination, that when Rosita stumbled slightly on the loose stones, he lost his balance. He fell heavily against the high pommel of his saddle, dislodging his whip. It rolled down the sloping path, stopping when it hit a pile of rocks. At the sound Rosita halted instantly and stood motionless as Juan swung out of the saddle. He scrambled down the path, his boots slipping among the stones and raising the dust as he went.

When he reached the whip, he found that the stock had jammed itself in a narrow groove between two rocks. Juan tugged at it a

couple of times, but it wouldn't move, and so, with an exasperated mutter, he braced both hands round one of the offending rocks and heaved. What happened then was to live with Juan for some time to follow. The rock moved violently, taking Juan with it. He flung out an arm to save himself and as he did so a mottled 'thing', like a thick blunted stick, coiled like a whip-lash towards him. Juan caught a horrified, fleeting glimpse of a broad flat head, unblinking cruel eyes, and a gaping, fanged mouth. The next second he felt a sharp stinging pain in his hand – he had been bitten by the snake!

With a sobbing gasp, he stumbled backwards, staring at the two tiny, blood-stained pin-pricks that were already beginning to throb and burn. Then his ankle turned, and unable to save himself he collapsed on the ground, spattering the snake with a shower of pebbles. Furious and hissing, it coiled in on itself, preparing to strike at Juan for the second time, while the boy, gripped by the most terrible fear he had ever known, could only lie in the dust, staring, like a hypnotized bird.

It was Rosita who broke the spell, as she hurled herself at the snake. Ears back and teeth bared, she reared up on it again and again, her high-pitched squealing making her sound more like a fighting wild stallion than a quiet, old mare. For all its speed the snake was powerless to avoid her trampling hooves, and after one last violent, convulsive jerk, it lay still, its back broken. Rosita, quivering and breathing heavily, stared down at her motionless adversary. If the slack coils had made the slightest movement, she would have reared up again. But the snake was quite dead.

"Rosita . . . . Rosita . . . . " The mare turned towards Juan as he staggered to his feet. "We must . . . . get home . . . we must." Already his hand was beginning to look bruised and swollen, and although somewhere at the back of his mind he knew he ought to do something to prevent the poison spreading, his brain refused to tell him what it was. Indeed his head felt as if it were stuffed with sand. Juan leaned heavily against Rosita's side, then taking a deep breath and making a great effort he reached up, and grasping the pommel, dragged himself into the saddle. Rosita stood as still as a statue, and only when she felt her rider safely on her back, his feet supported in the heavy stirrups, did she set off. She picked her way sure-footedly along the rough path, past the broken body of the snake and past Juan's riding whip. Only when she reached the flatness of the grassland did she increase her speed, cantering smoothly and steadily. Time and again she swung her head round to glance back at her rider.

Juan, sweating and trembling, was swaying precariously in the saddle, only managing to keep his balance at all by clinging to the pommel with his sound hand. The other hung limply by his side. He felt horribly sick, and everything swam before his eyes.

Then the thin line of the paddock fences appeared on the horizon. With a relieved snort, Rosita increased her pace, but as she did so, consciousness slipped away from Juan and he fell from the saddle. The mare jerked to a violent halt, and bending over the lifeless boy, she nudged at him with her velvety nose, whickering softly, as if to try to rouse him. But Juan didn't move, and Rosita, worried and uncertain, stood staring down at him, her reins dangling. She snorted again, throwing up her head restlessly, then, as if she had suddenly made up her mind what she had to do, she wheeled round and breaking into a gallop that even El Diablo would have been hard put to equal, headed towards the *estancia*.

Dolores, sitting on the verandah, deep in a book, jumped violently as the grey mare came hurtling up the avenue.

"Rosita, what is it? Where's Juan . . . " Dolores seized the mare's bridle, only to have it almost jerked out of her grasp, as Rosita swung round and tried to retrace her steps down the avenue

again. Dolores felt panic-stricken. Something had happened to her young brother, otherwise what was Rosita, excited and nervous and sweating from a headlong gallop, doing back on her own? The next moment – with the mare behind her – the girl was running towards the stables. Her mother and father had gone into town and the only person who could help her was old Manuel.

"Something has happened to Juan," Dolores told him breathlessly. "Rosita's come back without him. Quick, saddle Aztec for me, and I'll get Rosita to take me back to Juan. You follow in the jeep."

Within minutes they were off, Dolores on Aztec, her father's powerful chestnut, holding Rosita's rein, while Manuel followed in the jeep, a first aid box on the seat beside him.

For all her tiredness, Rosita forced a pace that made Aztec extend himself to the utmost, and Dolores, bending low over his neck felt the wind tear at the skirt of her yellow dress. They found Juan still unconscious, and Dolores's face became quite blanched when, taking his hand, she realized what had happened.

"Mother of God, he's been bitten," she whispered in a shaking voice, clutching at Manuel.

The old Mexican bent down and looked at Juan's hand. "Those are the marks of the Valley Devil," he said, using a local Indian name for one of the most deadly vipers on the *estancia*. "You must act quickly, *senorita* . . ."

Dolores felt sick, but her professional training took over.

"Manuel, you must help me. We'll do what we can now. Then we must get him home to a doctor." Her voice was steady now, and Manuel glanced admiringly at her as they set to work, while the two horses stood silently by. Rosita was utterly exhausted, and as if to comfort her, Aztec edged closer, and nuzzled her affectionately.

Juan was desperately ill for several days. Then, at last, the fever broke, and he fell into a deep, refreshing sleep, waking up to find his sister sitting by his bed.

"Hallo," he whispered muzzily.

Dolores smiled. "Hallo yourself, little brother. Do you fancy a drink of fresh fruit juice?"

Juan nodded. He was terribly thirsty, though he could not understand why, any more than he could understand why he felt so weak or why his hand was bandaged. Slowly he remembered.

"That . . . that snake . . . it bit me . . . Rosita killed it," he murmured.

"That's right," said Dolores, "and it was Rosita who got you safely home, too. Now, Juan, drink a little of this fruit juice."

The boy obeyed, and as his sister settled him back on his pillows, he looked up at her and said, "Rosita saved my life didn't she, Dolores? I was wrong to call her stupid . . . El Diablo couldn't have done what she did . . . " The next moment he had fallen asleep again.

When Juan was on his feet, the first thing he insisted on doing was going to see Rosita. His sister went with him. Rosita, sharing the paddock behind the stables with El Diablo, was grazing quietly, but she raised her head at the sight of her visitors, and trotted over. El Diablo followed her.

Juan patted his black colt's neck, but he flung his arms round Rosita's sturdy neck, and kissed her on her soft cheek.

"Thank you, Rosita, thank you," he whispered into her mane.

The grey mare turned and looked at him with her wise, dark eyes, then she gently rubbed her head against his arm. Juan kissed her again, and turned to his sister.

"You know, Dolores," he said with a laugh. "I thought Mama Michaela was just being foolish when she told me that the grey mare can be the better horse – but she wasn't after all!"

18

The Saving of the Speed Herd

"THEY ALL have to go."

"Every one? May Day and Eureka and even little old McNab?"

Jan Speed looked from her father, who had spoken the terrible words, to her mother, who avoided meeting her eyes.

"Yes, the lot. They eat enough for ten cattle. If we cut out every thing that is not essential, the farm may just pull through," Jan's father replied.

"It's a condition of this loan," said Mrs Speed in a low voice. "No non-productive animals to be allowed on the land."

The year or more of economies forced by bad luck and bad weather had not prepared Jan for the shock of losing all the beloved horses and ponies at one stroke.

"But, Mum, what about the Flag family?" she appealed.

"Fairy will be put down. The other two we'll sell. The ponies as well, although Ruth might take back McNab."

Her mother's words hit Jan like thudding blows. Suddenly her parents seemed like strangers to her. She ran out of the house, not seeing Mrs Speed drop her face into her hands.

Jan crossed the garden to a small field gate. The Speed Herd, as it was known locally, was turned out to enjoy the summer grass. Just now most of them were standing peacefully in the shade of the oaks. Only Banner, the ever-hungry four year-old, and McNab the Shetland with his coat of fly-proof 'thatch', were still grazing.

At the click of the gate, Fairy Flag, mother of Pennant and grandmother of Banner, started to lead the procession down to the farm yard. This was the summer routine they knew so well – turned out at night and kept in during most of the day. Only a frosting of grey on her chestnut muzzle betrayed Fairy's age as she walked with the elegant swing of a near thoroughbred. When she married Graham Speed, Jan's mother had brought Fairy to the farm. They had hunted together for many seasons, with time off for Mrs Speed to have Jan and for Fairy Flag to have Pennant, who had in turn produced Banner.

Nearly all the Speed Herd had just seemed to 'happen'. McNab, Jan's first pony, had been inherited from a cousin who had outgrown him. May Day, a native pony, had been rescued from gipsies, having been put to a cart much too young, and had rewarded Jan's care by becoming a clever, all-round riding pony.

Only part-Arab Eureka had been deliberately bought for show-jumping, and he had been cheap because he had proved too much of a handful for his former rider.

As Jan opened the farm gate, the little troop of animals passed her blurred vision as if she was looking through a rain-washed window. Automatically the horses made for the open doors of their boxes and the ponies for the old cow byre. There was the usual skirmish as Banner tried to barge into her mother's box, only to be firmly chased out again.

Jan shut the doors and then the byre gate. Folding her arms along the top, she dropped her head down on them and let despair overcome her – a slight figure in blue jeans, her wren-brown hair hanging round her face like a mourning veil. Soon hot breaths disturbed the veil. The ponies sensed something was wrong, but Jan could take no comfort from their concern.

"Oh, May Day, Eureka, what will happen to you? Who will buy Pennant and Banner?" She refused even to allow herself to think of Fairy Flag's fate.

Suddenly every minute became precious. Jan ran to fetch May Day's head-collar. Getting her away from her companions needed

considerable tact and effort. Ten minutes later she had saddled up
and the pair were riding away, followed by indignant whinnies. Jan
had no thought of where she was going, only the urge to ride and
ride and ride.

May Day's restless sidling along a gate brought her back to the
present and she bent to undo the latch. As the pony suddenly
whipped round, prick-eared and tense, Jan nearly found herself on
the ground.

"What's the matter, May?" she said, when she had recovered her
balance.

Then Jan heard the thrump-thrump of galloping hooves too.
Another rider was coming their way. Hastily she made another
attempt at the gate, for once through she could make a diversion and
so avoid having to talk to one who was most probably a friend. But
May Day was too excited now to stand still. Jan was about to
dismount when a girl on a black pony came galloping over the field.
She was plainly out of control. The girl's dead pull on the reins was
making the animal crane its head skywards, quite oblivious of the
barbed-wire fence that was in direct line with its headlong pursuit.

"Look out for the wire! Pull him round!" Jan shouted.

22

But the girl seemed past hearing and seeing as she leant right back against the reins. Answering Jan's squeeze, May Day bounded sideways, and the black pony, at once aware of May Day's angled charge, shortened its stride and started to skid. It was inevitable that horses and riders would collide, but as they were aware of it the impact was lessened. They came to a halt with May Day's head under the black's neck and the latter's head more or less in Jan's lap! The other rider slithered to the ground. "I'm still alive!" she exclaimed, as she looked up.

Jan disentangled the ponies' heads, necks and reins and asked: "Didn't you see that wire fence?"

The girl, who was plumpish with red-gold curls, merely gasped in reply. "Gosh, that was a near thing! How did you do it? Stop us, I mean."

"It was chiefly May Day. She knew what to do. But your pony needs a martingale," Jan said, adding to herself, "that is, if you hang on to the reins like that."

"He's not mine," the girl replied. "I hired him from a man called Jefferson."

"Oh, he's a dealer," said Jan. "I know him – he just hires out horses between passing them on."

"Then I'm sorry for whoever buys Ricky. He's a horror. I shall lead him back," the girl said, still from her seat on the ground.

"It's quite a way, you know," Jan told her.

"I don't care, I'm not getting on him again." The girl got to her feet and lurched. "Youch, my knee!"

"You can't walk far on that," said Jan. "We'd better swop ponies; May Day won't bolt off with you. My home is quite near and Mum can drive you back while I take Ricky."

"That would be super," said the girl, her spirits clearly recovered. "I love greys."

She had some trouble mounting but May Day seemed to understand, and kept rock still until her new rider was in the saddle. Then she moved off at a smooth walk. As Jan had suspected, the black pony only needed light hands on the reins to carry his head normally. Walking side-by-side, the girl told Jan her name was Cheri Grinstead and she lived in the small local town. She had had lessons at the Moorhill Equestrian Academy, but found them both expensive and not very enjoyable.

"We never went out of the covered school and the instructress shouted at us all the time. I think it must be like drilling in the army," she told Jan.

When they rode into the yard the Speed herd craned their heads over their doors excitedly, to look at the stranger.

"Do you ride them all?" cried Cheri. "Oh, you are lucky!"

"I *was* lucky, but not any more," said Jan, as her misery, temporarily forgotten in the morning's events, flooded back. Now she suddenly found herself talking about it.

"They're all going," she told Cheri. "We can't afford to keep them any longer."

Cheri's round, slightly cherubic face lengthened. "But you can't! Not all of them. Not May Day, she's divine," she cried.

Her concern made Jan open up even more, and she began recounting not only the circumstances of the calamity, but a mass of detail about the horses and ponies and their specially endearing features.

Cheri was a good listener, but at length Jan took a grip on herself.

"I didn't mean to carry on so," she finished. "I must put May Day away. Ricky can go in the old bull pen for now, and then we'll find Mum."

During the minutes while Jan saw to the ponies, Cheri stood thinking hard. As Jan was about to lead the way indoors she said, "It's perfectly obvious what you must do. You must hire them out to people like me who want to ride, but haven't got horses or ponies of their own."

"Have other people ride them?" said Jan. "I don't know if I could bear that."

"But other people will ride them if you sell them, and you won't have any say in how they treat them," Cheri pointed out.

"You're dead right," said Jan, staring at Cheri. "Come in and see if you can persuade my parents as easily."

So out of a chance encounter with a run-away pony, the Speed Riding Centre was born. Mrs Speed had greeted the idea with enthusiasm at once. Mr Speed had taken a little more more convincing. He foresaw accidents, unpaid bills and disruptions to farming, but even he gave way to the combined persuasions of his wife, daughter and Cheri.

"Give it a trial then," he grunted finally and retired behind the pages of his newspaper.

Almost immediately, THE SPEED RIDING CENTRE was painted on a board and placed at the farm gate. The name had been chosen after much discussion.

"People will expect motorbikes tearing round a circuit," said Mr Speed.

"But the name Speed already means something around here," retorted Jan.

"And Centre doesn't commit us to anything definite," said her mother. "It could cover hacking, jumping, general lessons – anything."

The first clients came before the paint was hardly dry, brought by Cheri. They were a sister and brother, Sonia and Nick Hatherly, of quite different characters. Sonia was quiet and just wanted to 'be with horses', while Nick was far more definite in his plans.

"I want to jump," he said. "We went to that Moorhill place and all we did was trot round and round over little low bars."

"They are called cavaletti," said Mrs Speed. "It's a good way to start, you know."

It was decided that Jan should take Cheri and Sonia hacking round the farm while Mrs Speed gave Nick a lesson on Eureka in the paddock.

"Don't let him jerk Eureka's mouth," Jan whispered to her mother before setting out.

"I'll fix him with a neck strap to hang on to," Mrs Speed assured her.

Cheri demanded May Day again, so Sonia was mounted on Fairy Flag. Jan was a bit apprehensive, for grandmother Fairy could still be uppity at times. But Sonia worshipped Fairy from the start and the old mare responded in the same way.

"She's like a race horse," Sonia said, admiringly. "Has she run in the Derby?"

"N–no," Jan told her. "But one of her ancestors won it."

Jan was riding Pennant, who was too much of a handful for novices. She was a little unsure about telling them what to do about obvious faults. Tentatively she suggested Cheri should lengthen her reins and Sonia should keep her heels further down, giving the reasons as she did so.

"A horse needs to swing its neck and head at free walk," she told Cheri. And to Sonia she said, "If your heels are down it helps keep your legs in the right position."

To her relief her corrections were accepted without question. They walked and trotted and had a sedate canter in a well-chosen place.

On balance the Speed Riding Centre had got off to a good start. And custom flowed in. Even McNab came out of retirement to waddle round the home fields with five and six year-olds; restful sessions for Jan and her mother between coping with over enthusiastic youngsters and nervous adults.

Some days after this a girl of about eighteen arrived at the Centre. She was very blonde and had small, hard features.

"I'm Margo Dykes," she announced. "I have ridden in the past, but I want a refresher lesson."

From the start Jan felt there was something suspicious about Margo. While Pennant was being saddled and bridled, her sharp blue eyes darted everywhere and one question followed another: how old were the horses, how were they looked after, what supervision was given to riders? As her mother was busy, Jan had to take charge.

"Call this a menage?" asked Margo as they entered the small field where beginners had their first rides.

"No. We call it the schooling paddock," said Jan, a little annoyed.

There was a growing atmosphere between the two girls and it put Jan on edge. The slick way Margo mounted Pennant and walked her round showed she was no beginner.

"Well, aren't you going to instruct me?" she demanded of Jan after a minute.

"Oh, er – change the leg," said Jan.

"Am I really expected to change leg at the walk?" Margo asked scornfully.

"Oh, I meant 'change rein' of course," said Jan, quickly. After a minute or two, she called out, "Trot on."

"Trot on without any preparation?" queried Margo. "What about collecting the horse and giving the correct aids? And on which diagonal?"

"You – you seemed as if you knew all that," defended Jan.

"That's not the point," said Margo, harshly. "I asked for instruction, and I do not feel you are sufficiently competent to give it. Have you a valid licence?"

"I don't think so," said Jan, caught on the wrong foot. "Do we need one?"

"Every riding establishment has to be licensed," Margo said as she dismounted and handed the reins to Jan. "I shall report you to the authorities. You can expect a visit from the council inspectors."

She strode out of the paddock. Feeling shattered and bewildered, Jan led Pennant slowly to her box, just as Cheri bicycled into the yard.

"Whatever was Margo from Moorhill doing here?" she asked. "She looked daggers at me. I guess it's because I come here now."

"That's it!" exclaimed Jan. "She was snooping! She wants to get us closed down."

When Jan told her parents of Margo's 'lesson', Mrs Speed remembered vaguely having heard of such a licence.

"I believe it's partly to protect the animals," she said. "Well, they can come and inspect. There's nothing wrong with the conditions of ours."

"Don't you be so sure," Mr Speed said gloomily. "The trouble I had with the council over the new milking unit! The stupid questions they asked me! You should never have started this thing."

Margo certainly lost no time, for the next morning two inspectors arrived carrying briefcases and looking as if they were on their way to their city desks.

"We'll look round first at the premises and the horses," said the one who was clearly in charge.

"Certainly. Come this way," Mrs Speed beamed, as if they were old pals.

"Mum can put on a good act when she wants," marvelled Jan.

The men prowled around, jotting down notes.

"That's just a cattle yard," one said, pointing towards the byre.

"Yes. But the ponies love it," said Mrs Speed. "They can be together and move freely."

Each horse and pony had to be led out separately. The men kept their distance and studied sheaves of paper, which could only have been supplied by Margo Dykes.

"Two of them are very old," they said at one stage.

"But completely sound," replied Jan.

"And one's only four. Not suitable for learners," the men said, knowledgeably.

"We only ride him ourselves," Jan's mother told them.

"That scar," one said; "was it caused during tuition?"

"No; it was long before we started the Centre," was the reply.

Finally they said, "It was illegal to start this place without a licence."

At last they put away their papers.

"We're not satisfied," said the one in charge. "There are irregularities. And we've had a complaint about the standard of instruction. We shall have to make another visit – perhaps several more. Meanwhile you must cease to operate."

Mr Speed strolled up as this bombshell remark was dropped. He looked so amiable that Jan believed he was pleased.

"I suppose you've inspected the grass mixtures in the pastures?" he inquired. "Recommended by the Ministry."

"Er – no." The council men looked a bit nervous.

"Oh, that's most important. And our feed formula? Fibre content, vitamins and minerals, carefully balanced to keep the animals in peak condition," Mr Speed continued.

"At the moment we're most concerned with the standards of handling and instruction," they said, trying to sound confident. But they were plainly floundering.

"Then you must certainly step inside," said Mr Speed, politely. "I can show you all the proof you need – over a drink."

The inspectors hesitated, then followed him towards the house. Jan and her mother exchanged astonished glances as Mr Speed led the way into the dining room.

"All manner of prizes," he gestured towards a cabinet of trophies with one hand as he passed them their drinks with the other, "won for all sorts of events." And then he pointed towards more cups on the sideboard, "You can't win all those without knowledge and experience, you know."

Jan and her mother kept an amazed silence while Mr Speed told the inspectors of past achievements. They were visibly impressed as they sipped their drinks. The final exhibit was a noble rose bowl.

"And how about this for all round excellence, presented by the

Institute of Hort . . . '' his voice trailed off while Jan and Mrs Speed became glassy-eyed.

However, the inspectors did not seem to notice. They put down their glasses and the one in charge said; "I don't think we need make another visit after all. Just fill in this form and enclose a cheque and you will receive your licence by return."

When they had gone, Jan said, "What happened Dad? You've never cracked us up like that before. In fact you've always complained about the herd's misdeeds."

"Oh, well I couldn't stand by and see what those dolts were doing to you." He sounded almost ashamed of himself. "I had to put my spoke in, despite what I have to endure from your animals."

"But it was a near thing at the end," said his wife. "I won that rose bowl for flower arranging, as it says on the side!"

Grani~the Pony of the Norsemen

"SOL! SOL! Where are you?"

At the sound of her friends' excited voices, Solveig Landstrad looked up expectantly from the jersey she was knitting. "I'm here, in the *stua*," she called.

She could hear running footsteps in the passage, and the next moment, the door of the warm living-room flew open and two rosy-cheeked Norwegian girls burst in so enthusiastically that the brightly coloured carpets, hanging on the wooden walls like tapestries, flapped wildly in the draught.

"Goodness me, a visit from you two is like a visit from a mid-winter gale," Solveig shivered, half-serious, half in fun. "I can see I'm going to need this jersey for . . . ."

"Oh, no you won't – not when you hear what *we* have got to tell you," Pillar Holberg interrupted, mischievously taking hold of her friend's knitting and tossing it on to the table.

"Hey, mind my stitches," cried Solveig. "I don't care for the thought of re-knitting that pattern again, not with three balls of wool on the go at once."

"It's all right, they're quite safe," Margrete, Pillar's twin-sister, said. "I wish I could knit like you."

In spite of herself, Solveig's blue eyes darkened fractionally. "Well, I do have plenty of time for handicrafts," she said . . . for Solveig Landstrad was a cripple. Both her legs had been injured in an accident when she had been little more than a baby, and although she could manage to walk a little by leaning heavily on the sturdy pair of sticks her elder brother, Jonas, had carved for her, she had to spend most of her time in a wheelchair. But she very, very rarely complained, and was such a sunny-natured girl that her friends called her Sol, after the beautiful maiden who, according to the old Norse legends, had driven the chariot of the Sun across the sky.

Pillar bounced herself down on the settle. "Don't you want to hear what we've got to tell you, Sol?"

"But of course," said Solveig. "What is it?"

"Well," began her friend, "we had a meeting at school this morning. Pastor Magnusson was there, and all the town council –" here she paused for effect – "and we're going to put on a pageant on Midsummer's Day, telling the history of our town, because this year is the nine-hundred-and-fortieth ——"

"Fiftieth," corrected Margrete, butting in quickly.

"Fiftieth," echoed her sister, "anniversary of St Olaf's visit here. It's Pastor Magnusson's idea, and he's got it all planned."

The town, where the three girls lived, was set in a green valley in one of the most beautiful parts of Norway. Behind it rose the mountains, and before it was the *fjord*, a deep, blue waterway that led out to the North Sea.

Although the town was small, it was proud of its long history. King Olaf I, who had introduced Christianity into Norway, had once visited it and so had King Olaf II, Norway's patron saint. When he had left, the townsfolk built a *stavekirk* in his honour, decorating the wooden church's steep, pointed roof with beautiful carvings. Margrete, Queen of Norway and Denmark had been there, and so, much, much later, had Fridtjof Nansen, the explorer, who had left his great Arctic ship, *Fram*, riding at anchor in the *fjord*, towering over the fishing boats. And then there were the many legends and folk-tales connected with the locality – all about trolls, witches, brownies and water-sprites, and about the Norse gods and goddesses – Odin, Frigga, Loki and Baldur.

"Oh, how exciting it all sounds!" Solveig cried, her blue eyes

sparkling when her friends had finished. "Can I book a really good front row seat now?"

"Certainly not!" said Margrete, and then smiling at Solveig's startled expression, she added, "You can't watch the pageant and be in it too, you know."

"In it!" Solveig's expression was even more startled. "But I can't be –"

"Oh yes you can, and you are," Pillar told her. "In fact you and Peer Erling are the only people to have been cast so far – oh, and Grani, too, of course!"

"Grani, too?" Solveig was beginning to wonder if she was dreaming this whole thing.

"That's right. You know the legend of how Baldur the Sun God and his wife, Nana, were supposed to have spent their honeymoon in the mountains here, and how they used to go riding in this very valley. Well, Pastor Magnusson wants to open the pageant with that legend. Peer'll be Baldur, you'll be Nana, and Grani, well naturally, he'll be your horse – he can't really be anything else."

"But, Pillar, don't be silly, I can't ride," said Solveig.

"You can't *now*," agreed Pillar, "but you will by Midsummer's Day. You're to learn to ride," she said gently. "Your parents agree, and so does Dr Thorsen – in fact, if you really want to know, it was his idea in the first place."

At that moment the door of the *stua* opened and Mrs Landstrad came in. She smiled at her daughter. "Now you know the good news, my dear, why don't you and Margrete and Pillar go out and tell Grani. It's still light enough for you to go for a short sleigh-ride if you want, and I'll have something hot to eat ready for you all when you get back."

Twenty minutes later, Solveig, warmly clad in a scarlet jacket and matching mittens, was out in the snow driving her two friends along in the attractive little sleigh that had once belonged to her grandmother. She was a very good driver, her father and brother had made sure of that, and on the brighter winter days the sight of Solveig Landstrad skimming briskly over the crisp snow to the accompaniment of tinkling harness bells was well-known. But although she could handle the pony expertly Solveig never drove out alone, and she never drove any pony but her own Grani, who, like his mistress, had been born on the farm. Mr Landstrad, as his father, grandfather and great-grandfather before him, was a

farmer, and his sturdy wooden farmhouse, with its carved gables, was surrounded by the barns that were the winter-quarters of the handsome cattle and goats for which the Landstrad *Gård* was well-known. But Mr. Landstrad also bred Norwegian ponies – the *Fjording* and the *Gudbrandsdal* – tough little animals, who, when they put their minds to it, could out-work Jonas's fine new tractor.

Grani was a *Fjording*, a descendant of the Viking ponies. His thick coat was the typical dun colour of his breed, and the eel stripe that ran the length of his back stood out as clearly as if it had been painted with black paint. His mane and tail were black, flecked with silver, and he had a small, neat face with alert, pricked ears and bright, dark eyes. He had been a birthday present to Solveig four years ago, and he adored his mistress as much as she adored him. Once Jonas had taught him to draw Solveig's sleigh, and her *stolkjaerrie* – the bouncy little two-wheeled trap she drove in the summer – it didn't take the pony long to realize that his mistress was different from other people, and needed his special care. Her mother and father used to chuckle at the way Grani would glance swiftly over his shoulder from time to time, when Solveig was driving him, as if to say, "Is everything still all right?" At the same time they were very touched and relieved by the pony's kind nature.

"We'd trust that pony with her anywhere," Mr and Mrs Landstrad would say over and over again, and when Dr Thorsen suggested that his favourite patient should be allowed to take part in the pageant with her favourite pony, they agreed at once.

Out on the sleigh-ride the three girls talked of nothing but the exciting event. Grani seemed to catch some of their enthusiasm, for as he trotted briskly along the broad path between the dark pines and the snowy silver birches, he kept tossing his head, so that his harness bells rang clearly in the cold air. When the ride was over, and the sleigh slid smoothly to a halt in the byre-yard, Jonas unharnessed his sister's pony. Then Solveig, leaning on her sticks, led him to his stall – at least she walked in front of him, and Grani followed her like a dog.

"I'm going to learn to ride you for the pageant," she told him, stroking his neck, and Grani, who already had his nose in his feed bucket, lifted his head, and rubbed his cheek gently against her shoulder, snuffling affectionately as he did so.

Solveig giggled as his warm breath came through her jacket. "Stop it, you're tickling!" she said. Then she leaned forward and kissed him on his mealy nose. "Oh, Grani, I can hardly wait for my first riding lesson."

But she had to wait – until winter's grip had been broken and the snow in the valley had melted to reveal the fresh green grass – and until Grani, who had not been ridden for some time, had, once again, got used to the feel of a rider on his back.

When, at last, the time was right, Dr Thorsen and Peer arrived one afternoon to help Jonas give Solveig her first riding lesson. She was ready for them – and so was Grani, who was carrying a handsome old saddle that had been given to Solveig by a kind neighbour. Made of yellow painted wood and green leather, the saddle had a high pommel and a high cantle so that riding on it would be like riding in an armchair. Solveig knew this was so for she had practised with it indoors – but now that she was to try it on Grani's back, she felt both excited and frightened at the thought.

"Hallo, Nana," said Peer with a grin, ruffling her hair.

"Hallo, Baldur," Solveig returned. She smiled up at him, thinking how well-cast he was, for Peer was a true Viking – tall, blond and blue-eyed.

Dr Thorsen shook hands with Jonas and turned to Solveig. "Now if you and Grani are ready, we'll begin. Jonas, hold him steady – although, come to think of it, I can't imagine why I should say such a thing, for your pony, Solveig, is the steadiest I know. Peer, go round to the other side and be ready to help her settle herself when I put her up . . . now, my dear, I'll lift you into the saddle. One, two, three – and up . . ."

In spite of herself, Solveig felt her heart begin to pound as Dr Thorsen bent down and lifted her from her wheelchair to set her on Grani's back. The pony stood like a rock, and as Dr Thorsen and Peer slipped Solveig's feet into the stirrups, she felt the comforting warmth of the pony's sides against her legs.

"Comfortable, Solveig?" asked Jonas, looking up at his sister.

Solveig nodded. "Yes, but it does feel strange. I seem so far off the ground, it's like riding a mountain."

"Some mountain," grinned Peer. "I'd be a bit insulted by that remark, if I were Grani."

Hearing his name the pony flicked his ears, and half-turned his head. Startled by the movement, Solveig gave a tiny gasp, and clutched at the pommel, but before Dr Thorsen, Peer or even Jonas could steady her, she had steadied herself, and was sitting straight and tall in the saddle.

Dr Thorsen gave her a quick, searching glance. "Right, then, if you are ready, we'll take a short stroll round the meadow."

Jonas clicked his tongue and the pony moved forward. At first, Solveig felt certain that she was going to lose her balance and fall – even though both Dr Thorsen and Peer had their arms round her, supporting her. She seemed to be swaying like a silver birch in a gale, completely out of time with Grani's steady walk, and for a moment she was horribly tempted to call to her brother to stop, so that she could be lifted down from the saddle. But then, shutting her eyes tightly, she took a grip on herself. To do such a thing would be utterly cowardly. It would also be insulting to Dr Thorsen and Peer, who were so eager to help her – and what would Grani think if he realized his mistress had no courage at all? So Solveig took a deep breath, and opening her eyes, she straightened her shoulders, and loosening her bone-cracking grip on the pommel, picked up the reins that had been lying slack on Grani's neck. At her light touch, he stepped out smoothly and proudly.

Three times round the meadow the little group walked, and then

as Dr Thorsen began to say that that was enough riding for one day, Solveig interrupted him. "Please, can I go round once more – without you and Peer holding me?" she begged.

"Of course, that will give me a chance to see how well you look on horseback."

He stood by the gate, and watched the pretty, slender girl ride steadily round the meadow on the sturdy yellow pony – the two young men by her side. Solveig had learned how to balance herself now, and she moved so gracefully in rhythm with Grani's walk, that it seemed almost impossible to believe that her own legs refused to obey her at other times. As the pony stopped by the gate, Solveig leaned forward and patted his neck with a hand that was trembling – just a little. Then she looked at the doctor. "Will we do?" she asked, her smile half-proud, half-anxious.

"Most certainly you will," said Dr Thorsen.

As the spring days lengthened, the pageant was uppermost in everyone's mind – and took up a lot of time, too. Rehearsals were held twice a week, some so bad that poor Pastor Magnusson was near to tearing out his hair and sometimes almost wished he'd never thought of the idea of a Midsummer pageant.

All the time Solveig practised her riding. She grew to love it, for the marvellous sense of freedom it gave her, and for the feeling of one-ness with Grani. And Grani's enthusiasm was as great. He only had to see Jonas, Mr Landstrad or anyone with his yellow and green saddle over an arm, to come galloping across the meadow to the gate, his ears pricked in excited anticipation, and his long tail flowing out behind him.

With Grani's help, Solveig soon became as at home in the saddle as she was in her sleigh or her *stolkjaerrie*. She rode quite unaided now – able to keep her balance even when Grani broke into his smooth, steady canter, and the highspot of her spring was when she rode to the summit of Sun Hill at the far end of the valley, where the wild strawberries and the delicious orange-berried *moltebaer* grew. With her went Jonas, Peer and Pillar and Margrete; Jonas and Peer on foot, while the twins were mounted on two of Mr Landstrad's brown *Gudbrandsdal* ponies – Anders and Kristin – who meekly followed behind Grani as he led the way.

Then, all at once, summer was upon them – and the day of the Midsummer pageant had arrived. The whole town was in a flurry of excitement. Announcements of their pageant had appeared in all the papers, from the little local weekly to the big dailies of Bergen and Oslo, and every seat that surrounded the wide green sweep of the open air arena on the edge of the town had been sold.

By five o'clock the cast were gathered at the school-house, transformed from their everyday selves by the skilful use of make-up and the colourful costumes.

Pillar and Margrete came running over to where Solveig was sitting in her wheelchair. Pillar was playing the part of a *draug*, a

mischievous sea-troll that delighted in teasing fishermen, and her brown seaweed-like cloak flapped round her ankles, while Margrete, as one of the ladies-in-waiting to Queen Margrete, looked immensely dignified in a gown of rich crimson.

"Hallo, Sol," said Margrete, looking at her friend admiringly. "You look lovely!"

Solveig, her long fair hair twisted into two braids, was wearing a flowing green dress the colour of young silver birch leaves.

"You look exactly as I have always imagined Nana," cried Pillar, her eyes sparkling behind her pointed troll mask. "But have you got stage-fright, Sol? I know *I* have!"

"Solveig looks far too calm and collected to have stage-fright," said a voice behind them – and there was Pastor Magnusson, a watch in one hand and a sheaf of papers in the other. "I have just come to say that it is time to start," he went on, "and as you and Peer lead the procession to the arena, Solveig, perhaps you'd like to go and get mounted on Grani. Peer and Jonas are waiting for you at the horse line."

"Oh, my goodness," gasped Solveig. "Oh, Pillar, I think I *have* got stage-fright now!"

"Nonsense, my dear." Pastor Magnusson put his hand lightly on her shoulder. "And I know that you – and everyone else – will be excellent. Now, off you go . . . "

Solveig smiled up at him, and then swinging her wheelchair round, she steered across to where Grani, with Peer and Jonas beside him, was standing as quietly as if he were in his own stall back at the Landstrad *Gård*. When he saw his mistress, his head went up, and he neighed shrilly in welcome. Solveig brought her wheelchair to a halt, patting his head as he nuzzled at her.

"Time to begin," she whispered.

Grani was already saddled, and Peer held his head, while Jonas helped his sister out of her wheelchair. But she did not need to be lifted into the saddle – now she could mount by herself. She did so with a graceful flourish that filled her brother with pride and made her friends look at her admiringly.

Then with Peer – resplendent in the golden tunic of Baldur the Sun God – walking beside him, Grani moved forward to take his place at the head of the pageant procession. Although he was only a small, yellow pony, he looked immensely dignified as he paced along. But when he reached the entrance to the arena he paused momentarily, and turned his head to look back at Solveig as if to say, "Is everything still all right?"

Solveig smiled at him as she patted his neck. And, satisfied, Grani walked on under the arch and into the arena – a pony from the legends of the Norsemen, who was carrying a fair-haired goddess on his back.

Moon Maiden~a Pony in a Million

MY FIRST memory of all is spring sunshine slipping through the trees and dappling my mother's coat with specks of gold. My second is of struggling to stand up on long spindly legs, and snorting with frustration when I couldn't. My mother nuzzled at me as I sprawled on the grass.

"Now, daughter," she said gently, "take it easy for a while. Just give your legs a little time, and you'll soon find you are running and jumping as well as any foal in the Forest."

I shook my head disbelievingly. But she was right, for, quite suddenly, my legs *did* do as I wanted, and then, almost before I knew it, I was trotting and cantering as if I'd been doing it for ever.

"Look!" I cried. "Look at me."

My mother looked. "You'll do, daughter," she whinnied softly.

As the days passed, my mother decided that it was time to leave the quiet glade where I'd been born, so that I could learn something of my Forest home. I was eager to learn, too, and soon, so it seemed to me, I had discovered three Forests – a heathland Forest, with pines and clumps of heather and gorse, a marshy Forest with willows and patches of bog moss and cotton grass and my favourite, the real Forest, with oaks, beeches, holly and yew, winding paths and secret glades. I met the Forest creatures – badgers, foxes, rabbits and birds – as well as the slow sleepy-looking cattle and noisy, bustling pigs who roamed about grazing freely. I had odd glimpses of the deer, too, slipping through the trees like shadows, and thought how beautiful and graceful they were. Then there were my own folk, the ponies, and there were two other creatures who did not live in the Forest as we did, but visited it regularly. They were called cars and people.

"Cars," my mother warned me, "are fast-moving, noisy things with squat powerful bodies and great staring eyes. They are safe enough when they are standing still, but when they move they are the most dangerous creatures in the Forest. You must never tangle with them for you will come off worst."

I listened, my tail twitching uncertainly. "But will they tangle with me?" I asked her.

She shook her head. "No, they won't, for there's one good thing about cars. They always keep to their own paths – those broad tracks where no grass grows. Cars belong to people, and people are creatures who walk on their hind legs. They're not as big as we are, but they are clever and quick-thinking and they know how to make others do as they want."

I didn't much like the sound of that, but I was reassured when my mother went on, "They're kindly creatures, generally, but you may meet bad ones now and again, in which case you'd be wise to give them a wide berth. Sometime soon, you'll meet my special people. They're called the Brierleys and they're real Forest folk – like us."

Spring turned into summer and my mother and I roamed the Forest happily in the company of a friendly group of ponies. The mares grazed quietly, while we foals played together. Sometimes, a few fawns would join in our games of 'he', but they never stayed long, for they were rather shy, and their mothers usually called them away.

It wasn't long afterwards that I did meet my mother's special people – and I met my father, too. My mother had told me that I was the daughter of Stormalong, the finest stallion in the Forest. He was a direct descendant of Zorah, an Arab stallion who had belonged to Queen Victoria herself.

50

"You're very like your father," my mother told me proudly. "You have his beautiful silver-dun colouring. Far more striking than being an ordinary bay like me."

"You're not ordinary," I told her, butting her playfully as I gambolled round her.

She butted me back, and soon we were having a marvellous game, racing round and round, squealing and whinnying and kicking our heels in the air. I was enjoying myself so much that it gave me quite a start to hear a voice suddenly cry, "Dad! Here's Mara and that filly foal of hers. She really is *beautiful!*"

At the sound of the voice, my mother wheeled sharply round and galloped across the clearing to where a grey-haired man and a girl with long dark hair were standing together. So these were my mother's special people, the Brierleys, I thought. I watched as the man patted her and she rubbed affectionately against him.

"Mara, lass you've done well," he said to her. "That's Stormie's daughter, sure enough. I'd know his colouring anywhere."

My mother tossed her head proudly, and whinnied to me to come and join her. Suddenly I felt a little shy and when the girl stepped towards me, I snorted and backed away.

"Leave her, Judith," said the man. "Don't rush her, that's a sure

way to make her nervous. Come and talk to Mara instead."

The girl did as he said and, to my surprise and annoyance, I found I was completely ignored! Even my mother paid no attention to me – she had never done such a thing before. I tried to attract her by neighing and stamping my feet, but it did no good. The only person who even bothered to spare me a glance was the dark-haired girl – and she didn't really seem very interested. Eventually I could bear it no longer, and so, gingerly, I stole across the clearing, until I was close enough to stretch out my neck and touch her arm with my nose.

She turned and smiled, and I thought what nice eyes she had. They were kind and brown, just like my mother's.

"Clever pony," she said, and ran her hand gently down my neck.

I shivered, for it was such a funny feeling, but, at the same time, it was rather pleasant, and friendly, too. I decided that I liked it, and nudged her to do it again. She did, and Mr Brierley laughed, and I noticed a pleased twinkle in my mother's eyes as well.

"That's a good sign, Judith," said Mr Brierley. "She likes you. If she develops the way she should with her dam and sire, you'll have a fine pony there in a year or so's time."

"Dad!" I heard delight and excitement in Judith's voice. "You mean she is for me?"

"Why not?" her father replied. "You'll make a good pair. She's got to be registered, of course, but her pedigree's impeccable, isn't it, Mara? Now, what do you want to call her? Pony's not a very exciting name is it?"

Judith hesitated for a moment. "What would you like to be called, pony?" she asked me.

I didn't know and couldn't tell her anyway, but feeling rather daring, I rubbed against her, as I'd seen my mother rub against Mr Brierley. I was trying to let her know I'd be happy with whatever name she gave me, and, in the end Judith decided upon Amberwood Moonmaiden.

I was very impressed by such a long name and when Mr Brierley and Judith had gone, I asked my mother what it meant.

"Amberwood's the name of Mr Brierley's farm," she explained, "and Moonmaiden, well, your coat is the colour of moonlight, isn't it? I think it's a very pretty name."

"So do I!" I said, and just then, through the trees came a magnificent silver-dun stallion. I knew instantly it was Stormalong, my

father. He greeted my mother affectionately, then turned and looked steadily at me. "Yes," he said, at last, "a fine daughter. She has your beautiful eyes, Mara."

"And your beautiful colouring," she returned. "Hence her name."

Stormalong flung up his head, his dark mane rippling. "I think it will turn out to be a name we'll both be proud of," he announced, and gave a triumphant whinny.

To the surprise and envy of the other mares and foals, Stormalong visited my mother and me a lot in the months that followed, and, on our walks together, he told me the history of the Forest and about its lore. It was very interesting, but I enjoyed it even more when he told me our history – the history of the Forest ponies.

"It's said," he told me, "that we first came here in the days of Queen Elizabeth I, when a great fleet from Spain, called the Armada, tried to invade this country. But the ships were wrecked in a storm. The sea is not far from here, and some of the horses and ponies – mounts of the Spanish soldiers – escaped and swam ashore. When they landed they stayed here in the Forest. It's a nice story, and some of it may well be true, but there were ponies here long

before the Armada. Some of our ancestors lived here before the time of William the Conqueror. Those ponies were known as the 'wild horses of the Forest'."

The mellow autumn days were followed by the cold and dark and windy ones of winter, but the thick coat I'd grown kept me warm in spite of the snow. Snowflakes puzzled me at first, and I'd bucked and reared as I tried to run away from them. My mother had laughed as she told me what they were, but she had been more serious when she taught me how to scrape the snow away so as to find the grass underneath.

"If this goes on too long," she told me, "the Forest folk will put out hay for us to eat."

I was relieved, however, that despite its beauty, the snow didn't last for long, and quite suddenly it seemed, winter was over. Then the first green signs of spring began to appear. Now I was one year old, and I didn't need to look at my reflection in the stream to know that I was no longer a tufty-tailed, spindly-legged foal. I was growing up; a fact made even more obvious on the day that Mr Brierley and Judith came into the Forest to collect my mother and me and take us back to Amberwood.

"You'll like it there," my mother assured me as she trotted

alongside Mr Brierley with me at her heels. She was right, too, for although I was uncertain and nervous at first, I was as happy at Amberwood as I had been in the Forest.

My mother was pleased. "Living here is a very different life to the one we had in the Forest," she told me, "but if you are happy you will find it very enjoyable. You like the Brierleys, don't you?"

I nodded. "Oh, yes. And Judith is my special friend," I told her.

"That's good because very soon, you'll be learning how to wear a saddle and bridle and how to carry her safely on your back," my mother said.

I wrinkled my nose. "On my back? Like Rob Roy does?" I asked her. Rob Roy was the chestnut hunter who occasionally shared our paddock with us.

"Exactly," she replied, "and if you want any advice, ask him. He knows more about riding than I – or your father, come to that."

So I asked Rob Roy. He looked down at me in a friendly way and answered my question so well, that when my first lesson on wearing a saddle and bridle came, I knew exactly what to expect. I could tell that Mr Brierley and Judith were surprised at my calmness, for

according to Rob Roy many young ponies hated the first feel of the saddle and bridle. I must admit that the cold touch of the bit on my tongue felt rather strange, and the bridle did tickle as it was slipped over my ears. But after I'd shaken my head a couple of times, and got used to the jingling noise, I found it quite comfortable.

The saddle was different, however – even though Mr Brierley did let me have a good look at the funny, lumpy thing before he put it gently on my back and buckled the girths under my tummy. For a moment, then, I was tempted to try and buck it off, but Judith's soothing whisper and my mother's stern whinny stopped me.

My first lesson didn't last long. Judith lead me twice round the paddock, and it was clear from the patting I received afterwards together with the pan of oats, that I'd done well. I really felt quite proud of myself!

I shall never forget the day I first carried Judith. At first I'd thought it was just going to be another saddle and bridle lesson – until I saw the sparkle in her eyes, and sensed her excitement. She mounted carefully, while Mr Brierley held my head. It felt funny to have even Judith's light weight on my back, and at first it made me hump my shoulders and skitter sideways a bit. Then I heard her

laughing and telling me not to be a silly, but to show everyone what a fine filly I was. Judith had gentle hands, and their touch on my reins told me clearly what she wanted me to do. Of course she talked to me too, and as we walked and trotted and cantered around, I kept one ear cocked back to catch her voice. When the lesson was over she slipped from the saddle and kissed me exultantly on the nose, telling me how pleased she was with me.

I tried to kiss her back. It wasn't very successful, and it made her laugh and splutter, but I didn't mind for I knew she understood what I was trying to tell her – that I was as happy as her, and as proud to have her as my rider as she was to have me as her pony.

A few days later, a sad thing happened. My mother returned to the Forest, and to my father. I was sorry to see her go, but as we rubbed noses in farewell, she told me that she would be looking out for me when I went to get my fine new shoes.

Her remark puzzled me, and even Rob Roy wouldn't explain it, not until we were both on our way to the blacksmith, with Mr Brierley and Judith. But, to my disappointment I didn't see my mother, even though I looked for her. When we arrived at the smithy, I forgot everything in wonder at all the new things for me to look at – the glowing fire, the shining anvil, and the clanging and hissing as the horseshoes were forged and nailed on to our hoofs. Rob Roy was shod first. He took it all so calmly, allowing the blacksmith to lift and shoe each of his hoofs in turn, without even a flicker of his ears, that when it came to my turn, I tried to act in the same way. The blacksmith was a friendly, jolly person, and his work finished, he gave me a friendly slap on the hind quarters, and told me that I'd been 'a good 'un'.

Wearing shoes made my legs feel strangely heavy at first, but I rather enjoyed the important clatter they made on the road. Then, as Judith and I followed Mr Brierley and Rob Roy down the grass track that led to Amberwood, I saw the two people I most wanted to see, among the trees – my mother and my father. They neighed to me encouragingly, and as I neighed back, Judith turned and waved.

"They're proud of you, Moonmaiden," she told me with a smile. "And so am I. You're a pony in a million."

I turned my head to nudge her in a friendly way – for it was the only way I could tell her that although I was proud to be a Forest pony, the daughter of Mara and Stormalong, I was even more proud to be Amberwood Moonmaiden – Judith Brierley's pony – and friend!

The Horse That Wanted to Change

CRUSHING the little pink and yellow flowers under his hard hoofs and twisting through the tall pine trees that threw magic, dappled shadows, the big brown horse journeyed purposefully up the lofty slopes of Mount Olympus. The gods who lived on the mysterious, enchanted mountain, found the cool peace of the afternoon shattered, as the horse trotted proudly into their midst. He looked neither to left nor right as he passed by them, for it was with Jupiter, the mightiest god of all, that he wished to speak. He knew that Jupiter alone had the power to change animals and beasts.

As he approached Jupiter's glittering, shining throne, the horse came to a graceful halt. With a toss of his silky mane and a flounce of his flowing, banner-like tail, he bowed his elegant head.

"Great Jupiter," he said, "I have been thinking a great deal about my appearance and I realize there are many ways in which it could be improved. In short, I have come to ask if you will change my shape so that I look more handsome."

Jupiter was astounded. To him, the horse was the most exquisite and noble animal that he had created to live on the earth below. He

61

sat back in his wide throne, stroking his long, grey beard.

"I can't think of a single way of improving your shape – of making you more beautiful than you are," he said. "What would you have me do?"

The horse stamped his hoofs in impatient irritation. "Well," he said. "For a start, just look at my legs!"

Jupiter did so, and saw only the neat sculpturing of the fine bone structure, the quivering muscles and the hard sinewy tendons that showed through the fine, sleek hair. "They are immaculate," he told the horse. "How could they possibly be improved?"

"They could be a sight longer," retorted the horse. "If they were twice as long, why, I could move as swiftly as the wind."

Jupiter nodded slowly. "Go on," he said. "What else?"

"My neck," said the horse, decisively. "It's so straight and thick and, well, rather undistinguished. I should like to have a long, narrow and elegant neck. More like that of a swan. It would look better with my new long legs too."

"A neck like a swan," Jupiter echoed. "What in the world is the use of that to you? But tell me, have you more plans for yourself?"

"Indeed, I have," the horse continued. "I would like my back changed so it will not take a saddle. I am sick of having such a cumbersome thing strapped round my middle, whenever someone wants to ride me. It's far from comfortable I can tell you! No, instead, I would like a hump on my back. My rider could sit on that and would have no need of a saddle to keep him in place."

Jupiter was beginning to find the conversation faintly amusing, but he hid his mirth behind his royal hand. The horse was so conceited and busy thinking about himself that he would hardly have noticed anyway. "Anything else?" Jupiter asked, innocently.

"Just my chest," answered the horse. "Perhaps you could make it broader. It's a little narrow as it is – not really quite impressive enough, if you know what I mean. Nor does it allow me to breathe as deeply as I would like."

Jupiter stepped down from his throne. "Have you thought how you would look if I made all the changes?" he asked the horse.

"Well, I've thought about it, of course," the horse replied, shifting a little from hoof to hoof. "It's a little hard to picture altogether, I admit, but I just know I would look truly magnificent." Here, he drew himself up, majestically.

"I shall do exactly as you ask," said Jupiter, "and you shall see for

yourself just how you *would* look." So saying, he clapped his hands three times and immediately a deep rumbling noise was heard. Then, picking its way clumsily through the pine trees, came – a camel!

The horse reared up in fear and horror at the sight, his eyes glaring wildly and a foaming, frothy sweat breaking out over his body. He looked at the strange, new beast – and there, indeed, were all the things he had requested of Jupiter. A long curved neck, very like that of a swan but not at all elegant; long legs too, but their extra length seemed to make them only ungainly. Above them was spread a broad, shapeless chest. But worst of all was the ugly hump that broke into the smooth line of the back like a molehill.

"There is your new shape!" exclaimed Jupiter. "Are you satisfied now? Shall I change you?"

"Oh no, Your Majesty, please, no!" the horse recoiled, still rolling his eyes in terror. "That is not at all how I want to look. Drive it away, I beg of you. Banish it back to the depths of the mountain. I never want to see it again!"

"Foolish, proud creature that you are," Jupiter rebuked him. "But your stupid requests have caused me to make a very useful and sensible animal. Its hump will allow it to survive in parched lands, where there is little water, and its long legs will carry it over far greater distances than yours will take you. I shall not drive it out of the animal kingdom. Instead, I will send it to the deserts of the world, where the likes of you would last for no more than a few days. I shall watch over it and its kind there, and it will be a faithful servant to man."

He patted the camel on its ugly head. Then he turned to the horse and said, "Now be off with you and never again let pride blind your mind's eye. Think yourself lucky, too, that I have let you remain the beautiful animal that you are and not changed you as you wished. But, so that you never forget what might have been, you and your descendants will forever be afraid of my new beast – the camel."

It was a wiser and more cautious horse that trotted humbly through the pine trees and down the mountainside, to the waiting world below.

William and Mary

ANTONIA VAN DE CORR glanced up from getting two *Suikerbrood* loaves out of the oven. "Mind how you go," she said. "Don't tire yourself, Jan."

Jan Martendyke smiled at his cousin. "Of course I won't. I'm only going down to see how Mary is – and William, too." He sniffed appreciatively at the delicious sugary-cinnamon smell that was coming from the two freshly baked loaves, and added hopefully, "Perhaps, when I get back I can have a slice of *Suikerbrood?*"

"It'll be waiting for you with some coffee," Antonia told him. "All our good Friesland food and fresh air will soon have you bouncing with good health again."

Jan pulled on his jacket, and went out of the neat farmhouse into the equally neat farmyard and down the narrow path that led to the pasture where William and Mary, the two black and handsome Friesian horses, grazed. He had been staying with his cousin Antonia and her farmer husband Paul, at *Genever* – or Juniper Farm – for nearly a week now, and already he felt a hundred times better than when he had first arrived. For Jan was convalescing after having appendicitis.

Jan's father had driven him up through Holland from their home near Rotterdam to the farm in Friesland. There the flat countryside, much of it below sea level, is dominated by two things – the mighty barrier built to keep out the ocean, and the pastures filled with beautiful black and white Friesian cattle.

"You know, Jan," Paul Van de Corr had said that evening after tea, "a lot of people believe that there are more cows in Friesland than people. When you're feeling stronger, Antonia must take you to Leeuwarden, our capital city. It's very beautiful, and in its centre you'll be able to see the bronze statue of a cow that was erected there many years ago. She is called *Us Mem* – Our Mother – and quite right, too, because this is Holland's cattle province. Why, Leeuwarden has one of the biggest cattle markets in the whole of Europe . . ."

"Oh, Paul, do stop!" Antonia had interrupted her husband, good-naturedly. "You sound like a tourist guide. Poor Jan, he's not up to such a deluge of information yet."

"But I'm very interested," Jan had assured his cousin, "because before I went to hospital, we were studying the Northern provinces, Friesland and Groningen, at school. Do you speak Friesian, Paul, because our teacher was telling us it is your second language, and I noticed a lot of the signposts were marked in Dutch and . . ."

"Friesian," Paul had finished. "Yes, I do speak it, and I'll teach you some if you like, so that you can impress your school-friends when you get back home."

So now, as Jan strolled down the path, he sang to himself, rather stumblingly, an old Friesian folksong. To his left and right Paul's fine herds of Friesian cattle grazed the rich pastures and some of them raised their heads to listen. The weather was warm and fine, so they were out of doors all the time, even, much to Jan's fascination, being milked in the open. But in the winter they were brought into the warmth of the big airy byres.

Mary and William's small pasture was at the far end of the farm – not far away from one of the narrow canals that criss-crossed the countryside, and beside the lane that led to the local market town. When Jan arrived at the gate he saw that the two black horses – who were actually brother and sister – were on the far side of the field. They were standing side by side as usual.

"Mary, William!" Jan shouted.

Both horses raised their heads. William, after a moment, lowered his again – more interested in grass than in a visitor. But Mary walked across to the gate, her ears pricked.

"Mary!" Jan called again.

Mary gave a low whinny, as if to say, "All right, I'm coming," but she did not hurry, for she was expecting a foal any day now. The Friesian mare arrived at the gate, and leaning over, she nuzzled at the pocket of Jan's jacket where she knew she would find some pieces of carrot.

"All right." Jan laughed as he patted her and gave her the carrot pieces. Mary took them daintily, her soft lips barely touching his palm, and as he watched her munching them, the Dutch boy thought what a handsome creature she was. Big and powerful, Mary – like all Friesian horses – was also gentle and good-humoured. Her coat shone like black silk, and there wasn't a white mark on her, except for the dainty white star in the centre of her forehead. But it was her mane and tail that caught the eye of everyone who saw her, for they were almost unbelievably long and silky. Jan knew that they were never cut, only brushed until they gleamed.

"No owner who really loves his Friesian horses ever crops their manes and tails," Paul had told Jan.

"With horses it is just not tolerated by the judges."

From the far side of the pasture came the brisk thud of hoofs as

William came trotting towards the gate, realizing that he was missing out on the carrots.

"Oh," remarked the Dutch boy, as the big black horse came to a halt beside his sister. "So you've come have you. Well there are no carrots left, I'm afraid – Mary has had them all."

But William wasn't fooled. Less polite than Mary, though just as gentle, he simply leaned over the gate, and pushed his nose right into Jan's pocket. A good-humoured scuffle followed, with William emerging as the victor.

Paul, striding across the far pasture, thought what an attractive group the boy and the two big horses made in the sunshine. Although he ran a modern farm with two big, powerful tractors, he still liked to use horses, for he knew there were some jobs they could do better than the best of tractors. He was coming for William now, and as soon as the gelding saw the farmer, his dark eyes brightened excitedly.

"Hallo, Jan. Want to ride back on William?" Paul asked. "I'm using him for carting today. No, Mary, not you. You're too near your time to work, now."

"When do you think her foal will be born, Paul?" Jan asked.

Paul ran his hand gently and expertly over the mare's sides. "Within the next day or so, I'd say. I think we'll have the vet to see you this afternoon my girl," he added, as Mary pushed her head against his arm.

But, for once, Paul was wrong, for when he and Jan took William back to the pasture, they saw Mary standing proudly beside a small black bundle lying on the grass.

"Good heavens! Here, Jan, stay by the gate and hold William. I think Mary's foaled." And thrusting the halter into the boy's hand, Paul ran across to the mare.

Jan watched how he slowed to a walk as he approached her – holding out his hand and talking to her all the time. But Mary was quite unconcerned. She lowered her head, and very gently nudged her foal to its feet. The little animal staggered slightly, but to Jan's delight it managed to stay upright for a minute or so before collapsing on the grass in a bundle of long ungainly legs.

"Jan, hitch William to the fence and come over here," Paul called.

Jan did so, but at the same time he wondered if Mary would mind, for he had heard that mares with newborn foals didn't really like people coming too close. He needn't have worried – Mary didn't mind a scrap.

"Well, done, Mary," Paul said, looking up to smile at the mare. "A really beautiful little colt. And do you know my girl," he added, getting to his feet, "I think we'll call him Jan, after your friend, here."

"Oh, Paul, thank you!" Jan smiled broadly.

"Don't thank me," said Paul, ruffling Jan's hair with one hand, and patting the Friesian mare with the other. "Thank Mary. After all, she's made it very clear that you're her special friend . . . Now, I think mother and son could do with a bit of peace, so we'll remove William for the time being, and as soon as we've told Antonia and everyone else at *Genever* the good news, I'll get the vet to come across and give Mary and Jan a quick once-over."

In the days that followed, the foal and his mother received plenty of visitors – and were delighted to see them all. Jan-the-colt, as he was known, was soon gambolling round the meadow, fascinated by everything – while Mary seemed to be positively glowing with happy contentment. But the same could not be said for poor puzzled William – who was so put out by all the mysterious

comings and goings in which he was not allowed to join that he was almost bad tempered.

"Feels he's been left out of things," remarked Jakob Hendrik, Paul's head dairyman, as he and his wife Beatrix were in the kitchen helping to prepare the *Genever's* entries for the Annual Dairy Market one warm evening.

The Dairy Market was a colourful and famous event that had been held in the square of the old market town for centuries. From all over Friesland farmers and their wives brought their milk, home-produced butter and cheese to display on stalls beneath brightly-striped awnings of red and green and blue and yellow. To win a prize at the Dairy Market was something every farmer and farmer's wife longed to do. Paul and Antonia had succeeded – and their awards had pride of place in Paul's neat little office.

At Jakob's words, Paul glanced up from the pile of golden-yellow cheeses he was packing. "Well, I can tell you this, he's not going to feel left out tomorrow, Jakob. For better or worse he's going to be in the thick of things."

"What do you mean, Paul?" Antonia asked.

"Well, I haven't said anything, because I thought I could get it sorted out in time, but the van's been playing up – and we're not going to be able to use it tomorrow . . . Now, don't everyone panic at once! Titus at the garage may not be able to get the van repaired in time, but he did offer me a marvellous alternative – with, I may say the blessing of the Dairy Market Committee, which is what comes of being its chairman."

"Oh come on, Paul!" Antonia burst out. "Stop keeping us in suspense. If we can't use the van how on *earth* are we going to get our entries to the Market?"

"By gig," announced Paul. "Titus has got a beautiful one in his garage – properly looked after and in very good condition. So what will be nicer than to arrive at the Dairy Market in a Friesian gig, drawn by a Friesian horse surrounded by Friesian dairy produce?" He looked round happily, obviously pleased by the amazed silence that greeted his words.

"You mean that William will draw the gig?" said Jan.

"But of course. Like all Friesian horses he's well broken to harness," said Paul. "In the old days most people around here would drive to church in a horse-drawn gig." He turned to look at Antonia. "Well, how do you like my idea? You're looking very thoughtful."

Antonia smiled. "I think it's a very good one. A gig drawn by

William will certainly have more style than your old van, Paul. But I was looking thoughtful because I was wondering about doing the whole thing really properly – with Jan and me dressed in Friesian costume. We've got them upstairs, you know. There's that marvellous embroidered jacket and trousers and broad-brimmed hat for Jan – if he'd like to wear it of course – and the dress with lots of petticoats and the *ooryzer* headdress with all the golden ornaments for me. Well, Jan, do you fancy dressing up for tomorrow?"

"Yes, *please*," answered her cousin with such enthusiasm that Paul burst out laughing.

"Come on, Jan, tell the truth, it's more the thought of riding behind old William in a Friesian gig than dressing in national costume, isn't it?"

"Well, yes," admitted Jan. "The dressing up will be fun as well."

That morning, the arrival of the dairy entries for the Market from *Genever* caused quite a stir in the old square – for they did not come in Paul Van de Corr's grey van, but in a sparkling high gig, drawn by a fine black horse with a flowing mane. The driver was an attractive young woman, the golden ornaments of whose headdress sparkled in the sun, while beside her, sat Jan Martendyke. The whip he held, which was decorated with rosettes, was only for show, for William, his good-humour completely restored, needed no encouragement to trot briskly. Antonia smiled to herself as she thought how William and Mary — and *Genever* generally – had given Jan just the holiday he needed.

The Cross~Country Run

"HOW MUCH more of this boring old dressage?" asked Nick Hatherley impatiently. "When can we go round the cross-country course?"

"When you've got the basic movements right at least," Jan Speed told him.

She was directing Nick and the bright bay, part-Arab pony through test movements in an arena marked by painted oil tins.

"You let Eureka lead with the wrong leg, and your transition back to the trot was dreadful," she said. "If you want to do well at the One Day Event, reasonably good marks in the dressage test are a must."

Sonia, Nick's sister, who was watching, said, "What a pity we can't share the entry. I wouldn't mind the dressage, but I couldn't face those awful jumps Nick likes so much."

"He's like Eureka," laughed Jan. "Wanting to be on the go every minute of the time."

Nick had persuaded his father to let him hire Eureka from the Speed Riding Centre for the local One Day Event. A light boy of wiry build, Nick had quickly established a rapport with Eureka, so that whether the obstacle was a spread, a horizontal, or of several elements, they tackled it with one mind.

Both showed relief when Jan released them from the arena.

"OK, have your go round the cross-country," she said. "But miss out the gully jumps. The rain will have made them dangerous."

"But those are just the sort we want practice over," objected Nick, shortening his leathers. "There's a coffin and a quarry at Fenton."

"All the same, skip the gully today," said Jan firmly. "I know what it's like after heavy rain."

The cross-country practice course had been planned by Jan and her mother, making clever use of natural features and field boundaries. It had not been built entirely with the blessing of her father, Mr Speed, whose main concern was agriculture. Now Nick and Eureka bounded away, Eureka changing in a flash from the rather bored, easily distracted pony of the dressage arena, to a dynamic war horse. "Now we're going places!" signalled his sharp ears.

A plain bar in a gateway was only the beginning of the fun. While

Jan and Sonia walked up some rising ground which gave them a view of a good part of the course, Nick cantered along the side of a corn field towards the next pair of red and white markers set in the end hedge. There was a ditch beyond the hedge, which Eureka took in his stride. The rail sleepers in the next gateway, a big tree trunk sprawling where gales had uprooted it, and a post and rail presented him with no problems.

Each jump behind them increased both Nick's and Eureka's exhilaration. Now they were going downhill and Eureka's hoofs sank deeper as the ground grew progressively wetter and heavier. Some poles across a gap brought them within sight of the gully jumps, sited in a miniature, thinly-wooded ravine. Here was where Jan meant them to turn right-handed through an open gateway and rejoin the course beyond the gully.

"It's not so wet," thought Nick. "And, we're out of her sight."

Eureka, who knew the route well, was already straining towards the gully.

"If it looks too bad, I can always pull up," Nick told himself.

The ground became heavier still as they approached the first markers in the cut-and-laid hedge. Beyond and below was a glimpse of the stream. It was usually little more than a ditch, but today it looked more like a thick yellowish torrent.

Perhaps it was not such a good idea after all, Nick thought, taking a pull at Eureka. But the pony had already made up his mind to go even though his hoofs were slipping on the slope. Nick's pull on the reins merely interfered with his take-off. He hit the firmly-layered hedge top and turned over.

Nick had taken tosses before – many of them – and had got up laughing. Not this time. As Eureka's head and neck almost vanished in front of him he seemed poised in space. Then, when he did hit the bank, Eureka came rolling down on top of him. Together they rolled on down, the world seeming a mass of tree trunks, hoofs, legs and saddle girths to Nick. Finally he was aware of the shock of cold water and a great weight pressing the breath from him.

Meanwhile, Jan and Sonia were scanning the thick thorn hedge, which was where the course came back into view.

"They should be back in sight by now," said Jan feeling a little anxious.

"Perhaps Eureka has refused somewhere," said Sonia.

"Eureka never refuses." Jan shook her head. "And if Nick had come unstuck, I'm sure Eureka would carry on. I think we had better get down in the valley."

Eureka struggled and struggled to get out of the stream. He was on his side with his forelegs doubled and jammed against one bank and he just could not get them free. His flank lay across Nick, pinning him against the opposite bank.

Between them, boy and pony made an effective dam. The water rose round Nick's neck, and although he pushed his elbows as hard as he could against Eureka, he could do no more than raise his head a fraction. Soon the water would be over his mouth, and then his nose. He had never been so frightened before.

Then he heard Jan's and Sonia's voices.

"Nick, Nick! Oh, say something!"

"No don't. Keep your mouth shut," ordered Jan, off her horse and slithering down the bank.

She saw at a glance what must be done and wading into the stream, she seized Eureka's reins, dragging his head round.

"Now try, boy. Up, up!" She hit him sharply with the end of the rein. With the weight taken away from the pony's bent knees, he was able to straighten one foreleg and then the other. Sounds of squelching mud and splashing water filled Nick's ears. All feeling left his legs as Eureka levered himself up. Nick shut his eyes.

Someone was tugging at his arms. Opening his eyes, he saw Sonia bending over him imploringly.

"Nicky, Nicky, are you dead?" she kept repeating.

"Of course not, s–silly idiot!" he gasped.

The feeling was coming back to his limbs and he was able to turn over and crawl his way up the bank. Sonia continued to tug at him even when they had reached the top.

"Oh, do stop it Sonia!" Nick snapped at her, getting to his feet with the aid of a low branch.

Jan and Eureka had reached the top on the opposite side. She, like Sonia and Nick, was coated in yellow mud, while Eureka was now a yellow dun pony with a dark head. His formerly plumy tail looked like a hank of frayed wet string.

"I'll have to break the jump down partly to get Eureka back," Jan called over to them. "You two had better go round the wood. Make straight for the house and ask Mum to let you wash down."

"You must have done just what Jan told you not to," said Sonia, as they squelched along, Nick trying to hide a limp. "You could have been squashed to death or drowned."

"Well, I wasn't," said Nick shortly.

"Eureka could have broken a leg," continued Sonia, relentlessly.

"And he didn't," snapped Nick. "Now will you stop talking about it!"

Jan was back ahead of them, having ridden Eureka, who, she was heartily relieved to discover, was none the worse.

"There are hot baths running for you both," she said. "Your mother is coming over in the car. She thinks Nick ought to have a check up."

Strangely, the bath did not stop Nick's shivering, neither did the hot drinks provided by Mrs Speed. When his mother arrived, she took one look at him and said, "I'm taking you straight to the hospital," adding to Mrs Speed, "How on earth did you let him get into this state?"

"It was all m-my f-fault," Nick managed to stammer. "J-Jan told me not to d-do the g-gully."

"I can well believe it!" retorted his mother. "You were always foolhardy."

"Some nasty bruises, but nothing broken," said the doctor who examined Nick. "He's in quite a state of shock, though. I'll give you a prescription and you must keep him quiet for a day or so."

Back at home, whenever he closed his eyes Nick went through the accident. It had all taken so long! It was like a slow motion film. In the night his moans brought the family to his bedside.

"No more riding for him," said his mother.

"He'll get over it, you'll see," said his father.

After a day or two the waking nightmare faded a little, along with Nick's bruises which turned from purple to yellow. But there was one thing preying on his mind – the Fenton Event. His father said, "It's up to you Nick. You must do what you want."

"I'm perfectly all right," said Nick, his voice somehow lacking conviction. "There's nothing to stop me riding in the event unless, of course, Jan decides against it after what I did."

Nick tried hard to keep the hope out of his voice, for this would solve his problem without loss of face. The problem, quite simply, was that he had lost his nerve.

Next day he went along to the Riding Centre.

"Oh, there you are!" said Jan. "Time's getting short. Eureka's all ready and keen to go. The fall hasn't worried him a bit."

"You're not cross with me for disobeying?" asked Nick.

"I would have been if Eureka had been hurt," laughed Jan. "You were a nit. But it did show guts, and that's essential for eventing."

Nick's heart sank into his stomach. Guts! At present his insides seemed a mixture of lead and cotton wool. Jan led Eureka out, saddled and bridled. The pony shone like a polished chestnut and pawed the yard, just to show how keen he was. Nick stood rooted to the spot!

"Well, get mounted!" said Jan, giving him a gentle push. "Today's your last chance for a practice. We've been feeding him up a bit, ready for the great day."

Nick mounted by the stirrup instead of with his usual vault. The saddle felt hard and slippery, although it had been thoroughly dried out and soaped after its soaking. Eureka tossed his head.

"Better concentrate on the show-jumping today," said Jan.

"Er, what about the dressage?" said Nick.

"What?" Jan gave him an oblique, searching look. "I was going to let you off that. Yours leaves much to be desired, but one more session won't make all that much difference. Anyhow, you'd rather jump, wouldn't you?"

"Of c-course," replied Nick.

Had they been alone Nick might just have confessed his fear. But Sonia was there with her friend, Cheri, and a boy called Clive.

Eureka bounced at the sight of the show jumps, on which the Speeds had lavished much brightly coloured paint. Nick kept telling himself they all knocked down and nothing dangerous could happen.

Nothing much did happen; Nick's heart wasn't in it, Eureka knew this, and several poles fell as a result. Jan kept shouting, "You let him get right under it!" And: "You're losing contact with him."

And: "Don't let him put in a short stride just there." Finally she said, "You're just not on the ball today. Let's hope it's like a bad dress rehearsal – meaning it will be all right on the night."

"Now, listen carefully. We must be at Fenton by nine o'clock at the latest. Eureka will need a lot of riding-in, and you've got to walk the cross-country course – that's vital."

At the mention of the cross-country, Nick nearly said then and there he couldn't go through with it. Then he thought of what Jan had said about guts. He just could not face riding in the Event, but his pride would not let him confess his terror. If only he could come out with measles, or slip off his bike and sprain a wrist.

Nearing home, he decided what he would do. He would go to Fenton at the right time and do the dressage test. Then he would even start on the cross-country course. After the first jump he would make Eureka refuse three times and get disqualified.

But with Eureka so keen, could that be done without making his part obvious to all who would be watching? Then he had a brainwave; he would lose the way! He had studied the rules and knew if he went on the wrong side of a flag without correcting the error he would be disqualified. It was as if a load had been lifted from his mind and he arrived home whistling.

The Fenton One Day Event arrived. The cross-country course covered both sides of the valley, crossing a sinister stream twice in the process.

Jan walked round the course with Nick telling him in detail how each obstacle should be approached and tackled. He nodded, making odd comments, and felt ashamed when she was taking so much trouble. The famous coffin very much resembled the gully jumps, and there was a horrible thing called the ski jump. A snake fence and a chikanor, among others, posed additional problems.

He had soon settled in his mind where he and Eureka would lose the way. It was to be at a single marker flag in the field beyond the first jump, which was a pair of harmless hurdles. But somehow he did not really feel relieved. Conscience kept telling him he was being a double coward – a physical and a moral one. Jan's cheerful assurance that he was going to do well made it worse still.

Back from their trudge round the course, he mounted Eureka and joined the bunch of youngsters who were loosening up their

ponies ready for the dressage test. Nick found it hard to settle in the saddle; his miserable state of mind put him out of touch with his one-time partner.

A snub-nosed boy on a hard, hunter-type pony came alongside him and said, "Haven't seen you eventing before. Gassy sort of animal, where did you get him?"

"He's not mine. I've hired him," said Nick, his hands full.

"Eventing on a hireling! You're hopeful," scoffed the boy.

"A hireling!" a girl echoed. "People will be entering on seaside donkeys next."

Just then Jan called out that it was time for Nick's dressage test.

Nick heard his disagreeable fellow competitors snigger behind his back. As he headed for the arena, he thought furiously: "We'll show them! We'll do a good test at least."

"My word," Jan greeted him after the test, "that was the best test you've ever done! What got into you? You had Eureka concentrating most of the time. If Eureka's up to his usual jumping form you're in with a real chance," Jan told him. "You'd better be getting down to the start for the cross-country."

Down by the starter the same pair were waiting to take their turns.

"Pleased with your dressage marks I suppose," said the boy. "But it's the cross-country that sorts out the good ones. Those part-Arabs are full of fizz, but they are chicken-hearted when it comes to the big jumps. Bet you won't get him over the coffin, if you get that far."

"Eureka's as bold as a lion," Nick retorted at once.

"Number twenty-six," the starter's clerk called. "You're after the grey." That was Nick's number.

Four minutes later the flag dropped and Eureka shot at the hurdles, like a jet from a flame-thrower. Nick was thankful he had dropped the idea of making Eureka refuse. With the pony so keen it would have been a shameful thing to do. As he headed towards the second obstacle – a trimmed width in a hedge – he realized it was also quite straight-forward. He'd jump that too, and get well out of sight before peeling off. Eureka strode over it.

The anger which had got Nick underway was dying down. Instead his heart began to sing and his pulse seemed to be in rhythm with Eureka's stride. Suddenly they were at the coffin.

"Take a pull three strides before, then give him his head and keep your hands down." He remembered Jan's advice.

Seconds later they were scrambling up the bank and jumping the exit rail to applause from onlookers.

At the ski jump they seemed to launch out into space, but made a smooth landing on the slope beyond. Seven obstacles later they were galloping flat out past the finish and the time-keeper.

"Any penalties?" asked Jan when Nick managed to pull up.

"Don't think so. He went like a bomb." Nick was in high spirits.

"Well done. The show-jumping isn't for half-an-hour. I'll walk Eureka round to cool him off, if you want a drink."

"I could just do with a coke!" said Nick as he jumped down from Eureka's back and gave him a special pat.

Nick and Eureka did a clear round in the show-jumping, where the jumps seemed very easy after the cross-country ones. When they came out of the ring Jan was talking to the disagreeable pair, only somehow they looked much nicer now.

"Congratulations," said the girl. "You'll be third for certain."

"Brilliant cross-country," said the boy. "I knew you'd make it, once you got started."

Nick stared at him. "But what was all that about hirelings and part-Arabs?" he asked.

"Oh-er, just a leg-pull." The boy avoided meeting his eyes.

"They've known Eureka ever since I've had him," said Jan, just a bit too casually. "But they like their little jokes."

Suddenly Nick realized he had been conned. Jan must have known, or suspected, that he had lost his nerve, and told her friends to goad him into finding it again. She would never know what extreme measures he had intended to take!

"Bunch of twits!" he grinned, giving Eureka a slap on the neck.

Tony~the Movie Star

ATTENDING HORSE AUCTIONS was a favourite pastime of Pat Crossman and Hank Potts and not surprisingly, for Hank was a stunt and trick horseman and Pat was manager of Tom Mix – the famous cowboy movie star. But on this particular day, they had been disappointed as nothing very much had caught their eye. That is, until towards the end of the sale, when the little black pony came up in front of the small crowd of prospective buyers.

"How about that one, Hank?" said Pat, as they stood leaning on the rails. "Any good, you reckon?"

"Might make out," said Hank, sounding dubious. "How much money have you got?"

"Six dollars," came the reply from Tom's manager.

"Well, if they're willing to let him go for $12.50, he's ours," laughed Hank, looking down at the six one-dollar bills and a 50-cent piece he had in his hand.

Luckily, the bid was accepted and the two film men came away from the sale promptly as joint owners of one little black pony that they christened Tony. It was agreed that Hank would take Tony home and train him for stunt and trick work.

Now Hank Potts was reputed to be able to ride 'anything with four legs' but he and Tony just didn't seem to get along, a fact that Pat Crossman was to discover when he drove over to see Hank one day and found him riding another horse.

"How's that little black 'un making out, Hank?" Pat called as Hank came riding over to him.

"Not too well," said Hank, shaking his head. "He might do as a double now and again, but I just don't seem to be able to get anything out of him."

"Want to sell out your share?" enquired Tom Mix's manager.

"All $6.50 of it?" retorted Hank. "Why, sure! But why do you want him?"

"Well," replied Pat, "ever since Tom's famous horse, Blue, died, he's been moping around the sets, giving us all the blues . . ."

"And you think Tony will cheer him up," interrupted Hank. "Sure, take him. Let's see what Tom can do with him."

90

And that began one of the most famous partnerships that the Wild West movie screen has ever known. Tony and Tom got along famously from the moment they first came together. They seemed to understand each other's every move. Tom barely had to touch the reins before Tony was leaping forward eager to obey a command that would hardly have been perceptible to any other horse.

Tony snorted with excitement as Tom saddled him for the Los Angeles rodeo that day. The bustling, noisy, colourful stadium was full of enthusiasts keen for a good day out. They were there to watch or take part in the day's busy programme of bare-back bronc and bull riding, calf-roping and cutting and other traditional events. There had been the usual spills as well as thrills, but nothing disastrous, and for the most part, the participants had enjoyed the tumbles as much as the spectators.

Then came the chuck wagon race. The huge covered wagons that had served as mobile homes to the settlers in the early days of the Wild West thundered down the arena, each pulled by four horses. As in so many of the traditional journeys, they were accompanied by mounted attendants, known as outriders. Today, Tom Mix –

famous movie star – was playing to a real live audience who roared their approval when they recognised him as an outrider on Tony.

The wagons raced down the arena at a gallop, hoofs thundering, harness jangling and canvas flapping, when suddenly and unaccountably, two of the teams collided. The driver of one of the teams tried to signal Tom not to come too close and to leave room for him to manoeuvre, when, at that moment, a second disaster occurred; a strap broke on a bridle of one of the horses harnessed at the front of the team. With a sickening crash and a confusion of harness, horses and men, Tony and Tom collided headlong with the chuck wagon team. The outrider and his pony were thrown against the rails and Tony fell, pinning Tom beneath him.

All was confusion, but within minutes Tom was being rushed to hospital, unconscious and severely injured. Tony, shaken and frightened, but miraculously unhurt, was led away.

From then on the tough little black pony stood listlessly in its stable, occasionally resting one of its white-socked hindlegs. Its small head, with the blaze on the forehead, drooped sadly downwards, and the pony showed no interest in its surroundings. Then the door of the stable opened and a kindly groom stood – none too

confidently – in the doorway, holding out a bucket of food.

The little black pony jumped to life, but not with pleasure at the thought of something tasty to eat. Far from it! Instead it made a headlong dash across the stable, its ears pressed flat against its head, its teeth bared and its eyes rolling viciously. As one already practised at such a move, the groom leapt out of the stable and slammed the door shut in a flash.

Thankful to be safe, the groom leapt back against the door. Then, shaking his head slowly, he said to one of his companions, "That's the sixth day now that nothing more than a few sips of water have passed Tony's lips. He can't go on like that."

While Tony was fretting in his stable, Tom was fighting for his life in hospital and finally, after seven days of black unconsciousness, interspersed with fits of wandering semi-consciousness, he once more opened his eyes to the world of the living. Just as Tony's thoughts were with him, so Tom's were with Tony. "Tony," he asked of his friends as they came to see him, "is he all right?"

Although Tom's friends tried to keep the truth from him, Tom sensed that something was wrong. Finally he was told that Tony was moping and miserable – refusing all food and attention. As soon as Tom's fears were confirmed, he refused to stay where he was, and despite protests from nurses and doctors, relatives and his friends, he demanded to be taken to Tony. Weak in body he might be, but his mind was strong and made up and he could not be persuaded to stay in hospital.

The reunion between man and horse brought lumps to the throats of many grown men, who would not have cared to admit they could be so moved. With evident delight, tempered with infinite gentleness as if aware of his master's weakness, Tony welcomed him back. And it was from Tom, the only person in the world the pony cared about, that he took his first bite of food for seven days.

Some time later – long since reunited in strength and friendship and with a score of adventures behind them – Tony and Tom were filming in the Santa Cruz Mountains. The film included a nail-biting chase along a narrow trail between the high mountains. The 'villains' had planted dynamite along the trail so that their pursuers, the famous Tom and Tony, would be blown to pieces.

Tom insisted on riding the scene himself, although the director wanted him to use a double. Tom refused. Where he went – Tony went. When he rode – it was on Tony. The director weakened in the face of such determined opposition.

With a wink and a wave to the man whose job it would be to set off the explosion, Tom mounted and galloped off along the trail. The detonator-man watched him carefully, waiting for him to get just beyond the point where the explosive had been placed. He screwed up his eyes to focus more accurately, and just then a speck of dust blew into his eye. In an instant he had flicked it out, but for a crucial moment as his eyes watered, his vision was blurred. The track was unclear but he was convinced Tom was past the spot as he pushed down the detonator plunger.

To Tony and Tom, chasing along the trail, the world around them quite suddenly blew up in their faces. They had been right on top of the charge as it was detonated. In a cloud of dust, flying stones and pieces of rock, the pair came crashing to the ground, Tom once again pinned under Tony's body. This time, there was an ugly, bleeding wound in Tony's side, which, along with his other injuries, should have made him roll around in agony. But where the pony had fallen, there he lay, without moving a muscle, his legs bent painfully beneath him. It was not that he could not

move – there was nothing obstructing him and he was conscious, conscious enough to realize that if he had struggled to get up, he would almost certainly have done further injury to Tom.

Not until Tom had been extricated from underneath him did Tony stagger to his feet. Now it was Tom's turn to show his devotion to his pony. Injured himself, he refused the stretcher that was offered him, and insisted on staying with the horse until a vet had given him a sedative. And not until the vet also assured him that the pony would live, would Tom allow himself to be taken to hospital for the treatment he so badly needed.

Sadly, all partnerships must come to an end and when Tom Mix – the one-time Texas Ranger, rough rider under Teddy Roosevelt, volunteer and fighter in the Philippines and Boxer uprisings, range rider in El Paso and finally, successful movie cowboy – met his death in a car accident, one of the most famous partnerships between man and horse passed into the realms of film legend. Perhaps, even more sad, no one has a record of what happened to Tony, but how comforting to imagine that he spent his remaining days in peace and serenity.

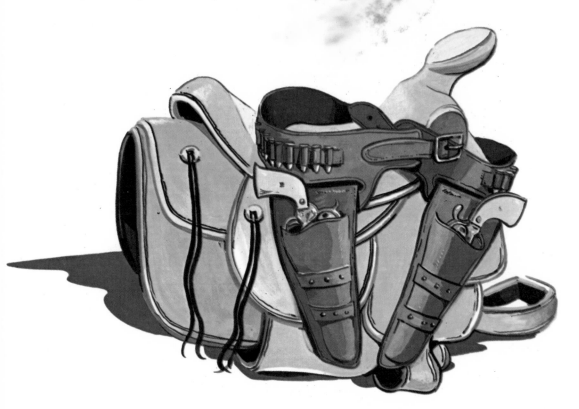

A Night Out

A LINE of riders zigzagged up the steep, rough track, climbing towards a towering rock stack. At last they rounded it and came out on a heathy plateau.

"What a view!"

"It's like looking down from an aeroplane."

"The horses can have a breather and graze while we have our lunch," said Jan, slipping down from Banner, the big chestnut four year-old. "They all had a drink at that stream a little way back. There's nothing to tie them to here, though. You'll have to hold on to them."

There was a bustle of dismounting, slackening girths and exchanging bridles for halters before the riders pulled out squashed sandwiches and bruised apples from their pockets.

The trek had started out from the Speed Riding Centre two days before with Jan in charge. Mrs Speed had the less exciting, but important task, of towing a caravan from one camping site to the next and preparing large suppers and breakfasts for the hungry party.

So far all had gone well save for a few minor mishaps. Clive, a dreamy boy, had let May Day step on her rein and break it. Jan had mended it with a handy gadget she carried with her. Eureka had untied his rope during a lunch break and vanished into a big wood.

The round-up had delayed them for an hour, but they had all thought it fun except Sonia. Sonia's devotion to horses in general always made her fear the worst. Just now she was fussing over her mount, Fairy Flag, an ex-race horse and Banner's grandmother.

"Keep clear of Nimrod," warned an aggressive boy with a showy bay pony. "He can strike if he feels he's crowded."

Charles Black, Nimrod's rider, was the only member of the party who owned his mount. His parents had persuaded the Speeds to include him in the trek as they were going abroad. He considered himself rather above the others and not bound by the same rules. Already they were a little tired of hearing about his show-jumping exploits and other daring feats of horsemanship.

"I suppose trekking is rather boring for you," said Nick.

"So far," said Charles casually. "But we might have an adventure. Might encounter red deer. The stags are very dangerous during the rutting season."

"We'd better get moving," said Jan, who had been studying her map. "We can keep on tracks and bridleways all the way to Addington. We've booked a good field and a camp site for tonight."

As they remounted to move off, Jan found Banner was lame. She jumped down quickly.

"Look at his near fore! It's swollen," said Sonia anxiously.

"He must have strained it over that rocky stretch," said Jan, feeling the leg, "It didn't show until after the rest. I'll have to lead him back to the road, and get in touch with Mother to fix up about boxing him home and getting a replacement."

"What about us?" asked Cheri.

"You can carry on to Addington," said Jan. "I'll give you the map, Cheri, and put you in charge as you're the eldest."

"OK, Jan. I'll see we all get there safely," Cheri replied, expanding with importance.

"Good place for a gallop!" cried Charles, as soon as Jan was out of sight, and thundered on ahead without further warning.

Excitable as always, Eureka shot after him, Nick neither able, nor willing to stop him. The others managed to restrain their horses.

"They can't go far without the map," Cheri replied. "The track divides into several smaller ones quite soon."

Sure enough they found the two boys waiting for them further along. "This way," directed Cheri, after a look at the map.

"This is the main track," objected Charles, starting off in a different direction.

"Nothing to stop you going that way," said Clive.

Cheri was relieved that the others settled for her route. Charles joined them, scowling. "Can't trust a female with a map," he told Nick. "Look, I've got a compass."

This impressed Nick. It was true that Cheri had not had much map-reading experience. When it was necessary to check the route again, she became a little bothered.

"I think we go right, along that sort of valley," she said a little hesitantly.

"You *think*!" cried Charles, scornfully. "You only *think*, and you're in charge! According to my compass, Addington is straight over that hill."

"And a compass never lies," Nick supported him.

"We could ride to the top of the hill and take a look," conceded Cheri.

It was farther to the top than she thought and once they got there, the track faded out. Uninhabited moorland stretched to the skyline. "We'll have to go back," said Sonia.

"What a waste of effort," retorted Charles. "If we cut straight across that valley, we'll hit the other track farther along."

It soon became obvious they were completely lost. It was useless to study the map, as they didn't know where they were on it. Charles's compass was no help either, as he had never really been sure on which point Addington lay from the start.

As they argued at each turning, the horses grew more and more dejected. Sensing their riders were lost, they became increasingly anxious over their evening meal. Then the tall pines around them made the approaching dusk darker still. Cheri was nearly in tears.

"It's all your fault," she accused Charles.

"You were put in charge; you should have taken the lead," he retorted unfairly.

"Fairy's so tired," Sonia worried. "At her age she could die of exhaustion."

"I've found some hoof marks," called Clive, who had been quietly looking around. "They're not fresh, but they might lead us to a house."

Without dispute they trooped after the grey pony, moving like ghosts under the eerie, dark pines. At last they were in the open.

"A farm!" Sonia cried, and they all felt the relief in her voice.

Through the failing light they could make out the single storey house and barn among the stone-walled pastures. A light showed in one window.

The man who answered their knock regarded them with displeasure, and it was nervously that they asked him to show them the way to Addington.

"It's a good long trek down to the road, and that won't take you to Addington," he said, abruptly. Then he pointed over the moor. "That's the way back, the other side of the moor."

"Could we telephone, then?" asked Cheri, horrified and miserable. "I've got the number of the farm where we're meant to be camping."

"Telephone! The nearest one's a box down along the road away," was the reply.

The man seemed about to close the door.

"Oh, please can't you help us?" begged Cheri. "Can't we stay here for the night?"

Either her big imploring eyes or the animals' lowered heads changed the man's mind. He pointed to a field gate.

"You can put 'em in there for the night, there's water in there.

And you'll find some straw in the barn. But you'll pay first. I had some campers recently who went off before light without paying."

Fortunately they had enough money between them to pay the fairly modest sum he asked. It was worth it to see dejection turn to delight as they led the weary horses into the field. The younger ones lay down and rolled, while their elders started grazing straight away.

The riders carried their tack into the barn, which was quite dark, and they bumped into bits of machinery before finding the straw.

The trekkers were so tired that even the discomforts of the barn did not stop them going to sleep very quickly. But Cheri woke early, just as a small window in the roof was letting in the pale morning light. She lay worrying about her failure of Jan's trust in her. Then a new alarm sprang to her mind: they hadn't checked the walls of the field . . . if the horses had found a gap they could be away over the moor by now.

She crept quietly out of the barn. Dew glistened in the early light and there was a smell of pines from the nearby plantations. It was with a sigh of relief that she found the horses and ponies were still there. But why were they huddled in a group, all staring in one direction? Cheri followed their line of gaze to a slope behind the farm where younger pines grew up from the heather. A bar of grey cloud was rising. Then she heard a faint crackling sound. Cloud? It was smoke!

Cheri's banging brought the farmer to a window.

"Fire!" she cried. "Over there, among the trees."

He came out in an instant, pulling on his clothes on the way.

"There are fire brooms up there," he shouted. "Get those boys out to help."

Cheri shook the others awake. They stumbled out, rubbing their eyes, but were quick to realize the emergency.

"The wind's bringing it this way," said the man. "It'll take the Forestry Fire Fighting Service to get it under control. But I don't like to leave to get down to the 'phone."

"We'll ride to the 'phone box," cried Cheri. "Sonia and I. The horses will go faster together."

"And Fairy is a racehorse," Sonia added quickly.

"You do that. Turn left at the road." The man was already heading for the hill and the boys were running with him like eager hounds.

Haste made the girls clumsy as they bridled and saddled Fairy Flag and Pennant, but at last they were mounted and cantering along the track, aware of an ominous glow now beneath the roll of smoke. The sharp morning air made their eyes run, blurring their vision. Suddenly they were faced by a stream across the track, spanned only by a plank. Wheel marks showed it to be a ford, but the mares treated it as a jump.

"Ooh!" exclaimed Sonia, who had never dared jump water before.

She was still in the saddle on landing as old Fairy Flag, reliving her steeple-chasing days, had swept smoothly over. Pennant made more of a bound, throwing Cheri higher out of the saddle.

The track was bounded by walls of rough, unmortared stones and, rounding a corner, the riders found their way blocked by sheep ambling along, herded by a man and a collie.

"You can't get by," he told the girls as the mares slithered to a walk. "You must wait till we turn off further along the track."

"But there's a forest fire! We must get help," Cheri cried.

She tried to guide Pennant through the sheep, but they only packed closer.

104

105

"You can't get by," repeated the man helplessly. "Can't hurry them either. The leaders are way out of sight."

"We'll be ages going at this pace," said Sonia. "What can we do?"

"This way," shouted Cheri, seeing a place in one wall where some of the stones had fallen.

This time Pennant took the lead, jumping easily. Fairy Flag stumbled among the loose stones on land, but recovered. They were cantering now inside the wall and could by-pass the bleating barrier.

Then a wall loomed up at right angles with all the stones intact.

"We've got to jump it. Are you OK?" cried Cheri.

Sonia nodded, hiding the faint fear that clutched her.

She saw Pennant arching her back in front as she cleared the dull grey stone. The gallant older mare thrust off her hocks and the air hit Sonia's face as she leant forward from the waist as Jan had taught her to do over the low jumps at the Centre. This time the landing was clear of loose stones and they swept on.

The bleating along the track faded and Cheri took a slight pull on her reins.

"We're ahead of the sheep now," she called. "Look, we can get back by that little farm."

There were cows round the farm which tossed their heads and charged away at the riders' approach. A woman came out and shook her fist.

"Get off our land!" she cried.

"We want to! Oh, please open the gate," begged Sonia. "There's a fire!"

Mystified, the woman did as she was asked. Wasting no time on saying more, the girls rode through and on. The sound of traffic above the mares' panting told them when they were near the road.

"Left turn," Cheri shouted.

"We can't gallop along the road unless there's a verge," said Sonia.

Suddenly there were the hazards of civilization – slippery tarmac, cars, lorries. Then a blue car drew alongside and a policeman poked out his head.

"Are you Speed Riding Centre girls?" he asked.

"Yes, but–"

"We've been looking for you," he interrupted. "Where are the others?"

"Back up there, fighting a forest fire. We've got to get to the 'phone for help," said Cheri, desperately.

"Stop right there," said the policeman. "We'll use our radio."

*　　*　　*　　*　　*

"We've had the police working overtime," said Mrs Speed. The fire was under control now and the trekkers were attacking a meal that could be either breakfast or lunch.

"First Jan getting them to contact me about Banner, then our SOS when you didn't turn up last evening, and finally getting the Fire Service." Mrs Speed shook her head. "I hope that's the end."

"If only you could have seen Fairy and Pennant over those jumps!" Sonia glowed with the memory.

"Nimrod would have done them easily, only I couldn't be spared," said Charles spearing his fourth sausage. "All the same, I'm glad I came on this trek."

Little Mohee

MARK SYDNEY burst into the ranch house kitchen. "Hi there, Birdie," he said. "Is Josh back yet?"

"No." His brother's housekeeper didn't look up from the sweet apple pie she was making. "Hand me the sugar, boy."

Mark obeyed. Singing Bird, or Birdie, as she was affectionately known, was a woman of a few words. A full-blooded American Indian, she was tall, grey-haired and dignified, and since the death of Mr and Mrs Sydney in a car accident eight years ago, she, and her kitchen, had been the real heart of the ranch house. Mark watched her now, his mouth watering, as she finished the pie and slid it into the oven.

"I've done my revision," he announced. "If I hadn't got the science exam tomorrow, I could have gone to the horse auction."

"Ssh!" Birdie stopped clearing the table and lifted her head, like a listening deer. "Your brother's coming, with six new horses, I reckon," she said, and then calmly returned to her clearing.

Mark blinked; he'd never got used to Birdie's uncanny powers of hearing. "I guess you can hear snow thinking about falling," he said in an awed voice.

109

Singing Bird's face relaxed into a smile. "Sure thing, leaves, too. Now, git . . ."

As he ran along the front porch, Mark heard the faint sound of hoofs on the track that led through the blue-grey hills from the highway to Black Horse Ranch. It was not the biggest ranch in the state, but the herds of white-faced cattle and handsome horses that ran there were some of the finest in America. Folks had voiced their doubts when, on the death of his parents, Mark's elder brother, Jocelyn, had taken over Black Horse. But even though he was only eighteen, he'd made a success of it, and now he was one of the most respected ranchers in the state.

When the horses appeared, Mark squinted against the sun to count them – sure enough, there *were* six! When Josh saw his kid brother, he urged his roan mare, Winona, forward. "Open up Number One Corral, Mark, so we can drive these fellas in," he called.

Mark dragged the heavy bars clear and stood back as the horses swept in, raising the red dust. In a moment Josh and Grey Wolf – the chief hand and Singing Bird's husband – were out of their saddles, slamming the corral shut. The noise made the horses skitter and squeal, as they bunched together, their ears pricked and their nostrils flaring widely.

"They're real beautiful!" Mark said, as he stared at them admiringly.

"But what do you think of your brother's 'make-weight'?" Bob

Gordon asked. He was a big Canadian in his fifties, who'd been such a lifelong friend of Mr and Mrs Sydney that their sons looked upon him as an honorary uncle, and loved having him spend his vacation at Black Horse. Bob Gordon was also a member of the Royal Canadian Mounted Police, his slightly bowed legs showing the years he'd spent in the saddle – for he was one of the officers who trained the Mounties, and their horses, for their world-famous Musical Rides. Now he dismounted from the chestnut horse he was riding at Black Horse Ranch, and threw the reins carelessly over the pitching rail.

Mark's eyes followed the older man's pointing finger, and he gasped in astonishment. He'd expected a foal – not *this*! Hollow-flanked and thin-necked, the dirty, dusty skewbald stood hunched and miserable, its eyes half-closed and its head drooping to its knees. Compared with the other animals in the corral, it looked a mockery of a horse.

"Good grief, Josh, how did you get him?" Mark said, but even as he spoke, he felt a rush of sympathy for the skewbald. He'd never seen any creature look so weary, so completely defeated.

Josh pulled off the old stetson he always wore. "He was the final lot, and when no-one bid for him, Old Chivers, the auctioneer, offered him to me for a few dollars as a make-weight."

"And your brother – being a softie horse-lover – accepted," finished Bob Gordon.

The next afternoon, his exam over, Mark raced back to the ranch and went straight to see the new horses. They'd been turned out into the small paddock behind the stables, and Grey Wolf and MacTaggart, one of the hands, were with them, moving quietly and confidently among the lively animals. Bob Gordon stood looking on knowledgeably.

"Hi, Mark." He smiled at the boy. "Exam go OK?"

"Not bad. I *think* I've done all right," Mark replied, as he leaned comfortably on the gate. "How do you feel they will shape up, Bob?" he added looking across at the horses.

"Pretty well, they're a good bunch, and that bay filly's the pick of it," answered his uncle. "Look how she's acting up with Grey Wolf and Mac. Like a girl at a barn dance, pretending to be above noticing the boys, yet having her eyes well and truly on them all the same."

Mark grinned as he watched the filly. She was a real beauty, but, even so, he soon found himself glancing round for the skewbald. He saw the horse, standing all by himself in the far corner of the paddock.

"Poor old devil," Mark murmured. "What a lonesome outsider he looked."

"He might be poor, but he's not old," said Bob Gordon. "He's only five."

"Five!" echoed Mark. "But he looks as old as the hills."

"Maybe, but he's got the teeth of a five-year-old and a horse's teeth can't lie," Bob Gordon replied. "Come, let's have a closer look at him." He led the way round the white-painted fencing to where the horse stood. "Lord knows what he's been through, but it's my belief that he has either been a dude-ranch mount for tenth-rate weekend cowboys from the big city or he's been in the sort of hick rodeo or circus that ought to be closed up for good."

The skewbald made not the slightest movement as the two

113

figures came up to him. He was either totally unaware of the man and boy, or he was too weary to care about them.

"What's Josh planning to do with him?" Mark asked in a low voice.

"Give him a chance, of course," was the reply.

"You mean he's going to keep him and make something of him?" Mark surprised himself, as well as the older man, with the excitement in his voice.

"Now, hold on there," said Bob Gordon quickly. "Josh's a rancher, and he's got to be practical. Like I said, he's going to give the horse a chance. But remember, when an animal's been treated like this, any one of three things can happen. He can become a killer – and who's to blame him; he can lose all his spirit and finish up broken and useless; or he can, with luck, regain his confidence and, with a decent new owner, may give human beings a second chance."

Half guessing what the answer would be, Mark asked which one he thought the skewbald was.

"If you want the truth, I'd say the middle." Bob Gordon glanced at the boy, and seeing him bite his lip, added gently, "But there's just a chance that with the right handling, he could turn out to be the last." He paused, putting his hand on Mark's shoulder. "Out of all the new horses, you've really taken to him, haven't you?"

Mark nodded. "Well, why don't you see what you can do for him," Bob Gordon continued. "Have a word with Josh, but remember, don't feel too badly if it doesn't work out after all . . ."

"No, Bob," Mark interrupted fiercely. "It *will* work out. Won't it, fella?" He leaned over the fencing and stroked the skewbald's neck, and to his surprise the horse didn't ignore him or even flinch away – he raised his head. The boy was sure that he glimpsed in the depths of the skewbald's tired brown eyes, a flicker of life and interest.

"Let me know how you make out," said Bob Gordon two days later, when, his vacation over, he was starting his long drive up North, back to Ontario. "But don't let him work himself too hard, Josh."

Josh grinned. "I'll try. But you know my kid brother, Bob. When he gets going there's no stopping him."

And there wasn't, either, for, as the weeks passed, Mark begrudged every moment spent away from the skewbald. He coaxed him to eat, making up feeds that MacTaggart swore smelt almost as good as Birdie's own cooking. He exercised him, walking him gently, and spent hours grooming him. The skewbald offered no resistance, but to Mark's bitter disappointment, he offered no encouragement either. He did everything he was asked, but he did it like a zombie.

"Well, Mark, he's certainly beginning to look a credit to you," Josh called from the porch one evening, as he and Grey Wolf watched the skewbald setting off for his exercise. "What do you think, Grey Wolf?"

The Indian ran an expert eye over the horse, standing indifferently at Mark's side. "He's a good sort of pinto," he said. "A 'painted horse' as my people call them. See how his markings run – the white beginning on his back, the spread of dark on his flanks. He's a *Tobiana*-patterned pinto."

"Of course." Josh snapped his fingers. "And the other pattern's the *Overo* – the one that usually has white belly markings and blue eyes."

Grey Wolf nodded. "But to us, they are all 'painted horses'. It was the Spaniards, when they came here to America, who decided that there were two patterns of pinto, and named them."

As if aware that he was the centre of attention, the skewbald sighed and turned his head. But there was no brightness, no interest in his brown eyes, and Josh frowned as he saw the flicker of concern that crossed his brother's tanned face.

"Only give him a short work out tonight, Mark," he advised quietly.

"If that is the case, I'll come too," said Singing Bird, as she came down the porch steps. "And I'll lead the painted horse," she added taking over the halter.

It was a still evening, heavy with clover scent, and as they walked along silently, Mark found himself counting the wild flowers in the paddock grass – the Brown-eyed Susans and the Laggard Roses. He'd reached ninety, when Birdie asked abruptly, "What is the trouble, boy?" Immediately, she answered her own question. "It's the horse, isn't it? He *looks* good, but he feels nothing, and you're afraid he never will."

Mark gave a gasp of relief to hear someone voice the fear he'd been trying to ignore for days. "Oh, Birdie, that's it exactly," he said. "I feed him, exercise him, groom him, but I can't get through to him or make him understand how much I like him. It's like he's behind a wall. He can't see me or hear me, and he doesn't even want to. Bob was right." He turned to the skewbald. "Come on, fella," he begged desperately. "Do something, please." But the skewbald never even moved, and when the boy looked into his eyes, he saw nothing but a shadowy reflection of himself.

"Mark," said Birdie, "you and that horse remind me of the old Indian legend about the young brave and his bride, separated by a great rushing river."

Intrigued, Mark asked what happened to them.

"They built a bridge," said Singing Bird calmly. "And that is what you and this painted horse must do."

117

In the corner of the paddock on Sunday morning, Mark finished grooming the skewbald. "You look a real picture," he told him. "Your coat's like silk, and, boy, how you gleam in the sun!" He ran his hand admiringly down the horse's soft nose, but as usual there was no response. The skewbald might have been alone in the middle of the prairie, for all the interest he exhibited. Mark sighed as he slipped off his halter and whispered, "It's all right for Birdie to talk about building bridges. But I can't do it alone. And Josh's going to want to have a talk about *you* before long, fella. But what am I going to say?" He sighed again, then bent down to pick up the brushes, beginning to sing softly. Too dispirited to sing his favourite pop tune, he chose a haunting little folksong about an Indian who loved a white settler. The song was called *Little Mohee*.

The boy was so caught up in his singing, that it was a few moments before he became aware of the rhythmic thud of hoofs behind him. He swung round, thinking it was one of the five new horses, half-broken now, which had broken out of its paddock, but to his utter amazement, it was the skewbald. Neck arched, tail lifted, he was pacing along with all the elegance and style of a high school mount, in perfect time with the song. Mark could scarcely believe his eyes, and his singing died away as he stood open-mouthed. With a snort, the skewbald trotted briskly up to the astonished boy, and butted him gently, as if to say, "Why have you stopped? Keep on singing."

When Mark hurled himself into the ranch house office, where Josh and Grey Wolf were working, the only thing they could understand of his breathless, garbled story, was that they and Birdie must come to the paddock at once.

Once there, he started to sing *Little Mohee* again, scarcely daring to watch the skewbald. But the horse didn't let him down, and once more he paced the paddock, swaying and turning, his eyes sparkling and his ears pricked to catch the music. Then he trotted over to Mark, this time rubbing his head against the boy's shoulder, snuffling warmly in his ear. Mark put his arms around the skewbald's neck, while Josh and Grey Wolf looked at each other in stunned silence. Only Singing Bird was unperturbed.

"Well, boy, that's your bridge," she said. "He's crossed it now."

"But why – how did it happen?" Once back in the office, Mark asked aloud the question that he had been asking himself over and over.

Josh smiled across at his brother. "We'll never really know, but I guess he was a high school horse, who, for some reason, hit a bad patch. The only way he could cope was to shut off – completely – until he heard you singing what must be one of his working tunes. It reminded him of what must have been a happy time in his life, and as Birdie said, it helped him across his bridge."

"Do you think he'll make a Black Horse cowpony?" Mark asked.

"I doubt it," was Josh's reply. "But I'll tell you one thing, Mark, when you've finished working on him, and you've got a long way to go yet, you'll have a fine saddle horse there. And if you treat him really good and gently, you might even be able to get him to give us *Little Mohee* at the next state Show in the fall, with you on top." Josh laughed at the smile that crossed his kid brother's face. "Come on, let's go and see him again, and take an apple for him, too."

The skewbald didn't see them arrive, for he was grazing with his back to the paddock gate.

"Here, fella!" Mark shouted, his voice shaking with excitement – and fear – lest the events of the morning had just been a lucky break. But, at the sound of his voice the skewbald twitched his ears, and glanced round. He hesitated for a moment, then came – not at a walk or a trot – but at a swift, graceful canter, and when he arrived he thrust his head over the gate, and nuzzled gently at Mark.

"What do you plan to call him?" Josh asked, as he watched the boy and the horse share the rosy apple.

"Why, *Little Mohee*, of course. What else?" laughed his kid brother. Little Mohee gave a low, satisfied whinny, as if in agreement with the name his new master had just given him.

Good~bye, Bess

THE COAL-BLACK mare galloped through the night, every fibre of her body ready to obey her fearless rider's instant command. The moon, peeping occasionally from behind formless, black clouds, could not pick out a single white hair on her ebony coat to betray her presence. Merging as she did with the darkness around her, she was a perfect companion to the night, and it was fitting that this, her final journey, should be undertaken through the long, sleeping, night hours.

Her rider too, was in perfect harmony, both with her and the dark lanes and fields through which he rode her ceaselessly. His black hat and breeches, eye-mask and long flowing cloak, were the tell-tale clothes of his livelihood, but they too, made it hard to pick him out against the night's eerie shadows. He was the most infamous highwayman of all time – Dick Turpin. A man whose name is never uttered, without thinking too of Black Bess, the brave little mare, who, time and again, carried him safely away from his pursuers.

Black Bess was the daughter of a desert Arab and an English thoroughbred racehorse, and from them she inherited a fiery, but

121

gentle, temperament, indomitable strength and tireless stamina, a willing spirit and a fleetness of foot that was essential to one who lived constantly outside the law. Small she may have been, but she was perfectly formed. She held her finely shaped head high in the air, her alert, pricked ears and her brightly shining eyes always ready to sense danger. At the merest hint of something unusual, she would snort through her broadly flaring nostrils, arch her clean neck and paw impatiently at the ground with her finely sculptured hoofs. Every nerve and sinew in her body was tense; every muscle that rippled beneath her coat's glossy surface was taut – ready to flee to some safer spot, however far away it might be.

Black Bess and Dick Turpin had dodged their pursuers on many occasions, outwitting them by standing stock-still and silent, wrapped in the cloak of night behind a high hedge, or more generally, by outpacing them. But tonight, they were to tackle together a journey longer than ever before; one that most people would have said was impossible; one that even Dick Turpin would only have undertaken if there had been no alternative.

As on so many other early evenings, the lawless pair were galloping across the fields and tracks that, in those days, were the outlying lands of the City of London. Three officers of the law were on their tail, but sufficiently far behind for him to take rein. Earlier that evening, indeed as a forerunner to the chase, Dick Turpin had seen a friend and fellow highwayman shot by one of the constables and on reflection, he realized he had few friends left who would help him in London. But, where else were there people who would give him support? The only place was York – 200 miles north of London!

"Bess, my lass," he said, as he gathered up the reins. "Prepare yourself, for it is to York we are going." And as if she understood, the faithful mare whinnied softly in response, already moving steadily across the turf.

It was a crazy and desperate scheme, for no horse can be expected to travel such a distance in one night – not even one of Black Bess's strength and determination. But for Dick Turpin there seemed to be no other course. It has to be said too, that it appealed to his highwayman's sense of romance and danger!

Together they headed north, across the gorse-covered heathland, and avenues lined with tall pine trees. Pursuers and pursued kept pace with one another, neither gaining, nor losing, any

ground. Soon they reached a village and the sound of Bess's hoofs clattering over the cobbled streets, brought the villagers away from their evening meals, to their doors and windows.

Cries of "A highwayman! A highwayman!" were soon echoing down the street, followed by "Stop him! Stop him!" Three horsemen appeared in front of Dick, but at the sight of him, his reins now between his teeth and a pistol in each hand, they took little time in deciding that discretion was the better part of their valour!

Turpin's pursuers, however, were suddenly jubilant, for at the other end of the village was a toll-gate, and its keeper, who must have been alerted by the cries, would surely not open it to let the wild rider through. Indeed he did not, and nor indeed did he need to, for Dick rode Bess straight at the gate without slowing her down for an instant. Like a bird, she rose into the air and the gate was way beneath her. The next moment the pair had disappeared into the dark countryside ahead.

Arriving at the gate on panting, puffing horses, the constables shouted at the astonished keeper, "Open the gate, man. Quickly! Don't stand there while Turpin rides on!"

"Not until you pay the fee will I open it," retorted the keeper. "It seems I've missed my dues once already tonight. And I don't intend to be done out of them a second time!"

"Can't you see that was a highwayman?" an exasperated officer replied. "We are officers of the law. Now open the gate!"

"Not until you pay," said the keeper resolutely. And he stood his ground firmly, refusing to move.

Amid much cursing, the officer thrust a coin into the keeper's waiting hand, and as he slowly opened the gate, the riders shot through.

Dick Turpin had now gained a fair amount of ground over his pursuers and he paused to give Black Bess a quick rest to regain her breath, before riding her through the next village. Here once again, the street was soon full of people, shouting and waving their arms and throwing things at the headlong pair. So swiftly did they pass however, that none was to find its mark.

Towards the end of the street, a man and his donkey cart, returning late from their day's work were crossing the road. With no time to go round them and no hope of pulling up, Dick Turpin and Black Bess treated the pair as they had done the toll-gate before them. The poor man might well have been excused for thinking it was the devil himself who soared over him in the dusky gloom of approaching night.

On and on galloped Dick and Black Bess, and after them, just as relentlessly, their pursuers followed. The usually peaceful evening sounds of the countryside – the low hoot of the night owl, and the contented lowing of the cattle as they chewed the cud – were lost in the pounding of hoofs and the horses' laboured breath. No longer did the officers shout at their quarry, more intent now on saving their energies for the chase.

Inspired by the intoxicating speed, the thrill of the danger and the strong, rythmic pace of the little mare beneath him, Dick was in high spirits.

"Perhaps one day they will catch me," he thought to himself. "But then, as now, I will be a man who is not afraid to die. A man who has never turned his back on a friend. Until that time, though, I'll give them something to talk about!"

Then, leaning forward in the saddle, he said out loud, "Bess, my girl, this ride of ours will live on long after we are both dead and buried. It will be talked about far and wide, and your name will be linked with mine for ever. We shall be remembered together!"

Then again, he thought to himself, "What if it should be too

much. Can she really keep going for such a distance? What if . . .?"

Out loud once more, he said, "If it comes to it, it is better that you die now, with me by your side, than fall into the knacker's hands or end your days pulling a grocer's cart, if they should catch me. Forward, Bess, together we'll reach York!"

Through dark, eerie woods, flint-filled fields and ploughed pastures, sweeping plains and moonlit valleys, they strode on, clearing hedges and gates that obstructed their path. Occasionally the clatter of Bess's hoofs would resound with a hollow ring as they rode across a low bridge or through the now-deserted streets of a town or village. Three counties lay behind them before they paused for any appreciable rest.

Meanwhile the persistent officers kept up the chase, receiving word along the route of which direction Dick and Bess had taken, and that their destination was York. They, however, did not confine themselves to the tireless efforts of just one horse apiece. Instead, at each post-house they passed, they stopped to change on to fresh mounts. Thus they were never far behind Dick Turpin and Black Bess.

After some six or seven hours, Dick Turpin was nearing a small inn which was known to him. The boy who looked after the horses there had been an acquaintance of his and it seemed a fine place to

stop for a short respite. As Dick knocked on the stable door, the tousled head of a young boy appeared out of an open window.

"Why, hallo, Mr Turpin," the boy said. "Nice to see you. Is there something I can do for you?"

"There is indeed," said Dick, already out of the saddle and loosening the girth round Black Bess's heaving sides. "Get me two bottles of brandy and a piece of raw steak. No, make it three bottles, and fetch me a pail of water too."

"Right away," said the lad, and as he went, he said to himself, "Three bottles of brandy and a bucket of water to wash down a raw steak. My word, I've heard it said such men are made of strong stuff, but now I have proof of it!"

Dick led the gallant little mare into the stable and removed her saddle and bridle altogether. No groom could have been more fastidious in the attention he gave her. He scraped the sweat off her foaming body and rubbed her all over with wisps of clean, dry straw. He ran his hands down each hard leg, to make sure there were no cuts or injuries that would indicate they were feeling the strain of the mad ride. He checked each foot to see no stone or piece of flint had become lodged to dig into the sensitive sole and to make sure the shoes were still in place with no nails working loose.

The lad had returned with the brandy and steak meanwhile, but he was to be even more surprised at the use to which Dick put them. Taking no more than a thimbleful from one of the bottles to fortify himself, he tipped the rest into the bucket of water and this he used to wash down Bess from head to foot! The raw steak, far from satisfying any pangs of hunger he may have felt, he rubbed round and round and over and over the bit of Bess's bridle. "Now she will go like the wind as long as there's breath in her body," he said. Then he replaced the saddle and bridle.

The next moment, Bess was tossing her head and pawing the ground, as if eager to be off. Even Dick, who was used to his little mare's willingness and keenness was surprised at such seemingly inexhaustible strength.

He led her dancing and prancing, out into the open. As he leapt lightly into the saddle, Bess lifted her head and pricked up her ears. In the near distance, they could hear the sound of hoof beats.

"They are coming," said Dick.

"Who are coming?" echoed the lad.

Without answering his question, Dick Turpin said, "The road

bends here doesn't it, going round to the right? But what lies behind that shed?" And he pointed to a small building as he talked.

"A high fence, Sir," answered the lad. "And immediately beyond it is a steep hill. No horse could possibly go down it and still be on its feet when it reached the bottom."

Even as they spoke, Dick's pursuers were rounding the bend of the road, so that, should he have set off along it, pursuer and pursued would have ridden headlong into one another.

"Come into the stable, Sir," said the lad. "It's your only chance."

Failing to see how such a move would save him, Dick Turpin had no alternative but to do as the lad said and he urged Bess through the open door. The lad slammed and bolted it behind him, just as the constable was approaching it.

"Now we have you," shouted the leader of Dick's pursuers. "Open the door, for there is no way you can escape."

With that, the stable lad thrust his head through the window, just as he had done on Dick's arrival. "What is it you want, Constable?" he asked. "There's no one here but me, and we have no quarrel."

"Do you think I am stupid, boy?" asked the constable, already off his horse and preparing to kick open the door. The lad saved him the trouble by opening it and the three officers rushed in. The lad was telling the truth. There was no one there!

Seeing an open door at the back, the officers ran to it. The ground outside fell away in a steep slope that was like the sides of a ravine. No sensible horseman would have put his horse to it, and yet there were freshly made hoof-prints on the soft turf. Way below, they could just make out the figure of a horseman, his cloak flying out behind him.

"There he goes!" the chief officer cried. "By heaven, the man's a villain to be sure, but for all that he is a fine horseman! I have half a mind to give up the chase now. But duty calls and justice must be done."

"I doubt if I shall be able to sit down in comfort for a week after this," mumbled one of his colleagues as they remounted and set off along the road once more.

With two more counties behind them, Bess's step was beginning to falter, her head was a little lower and her breath a little more laboured. As the night enveloped the pair, and they continued past the hedges and fields, low houses and tall church spires, not one bit of her willing spirit left Bess, but the flesh was undoubtedly weaker. Already she had done more than any horse should be asked

to do. Dick Turpin was aware of these failing signs and was deeply distressed by them, but he dared not check her, lest in doing so, she should miss her stride and fall, perhaps never to rise again.

As the grey dawn began to creep quietly in across the sky and the early morning mists swirled silently above the fields, Bess suddenly floundered and fell, throwing her rider on to the ground in front. Instantly she was up, bending over him as if in apology, before he had time to rise. But her eyes were staring wildly and her sides were heaving in laboured pants.

"Poor Bess," said Dick Turpin, speaking to her softly, fondling her head and passing his hand over her to see if she had hurt herself in the fall. "I shouldn't have asked so much of you, you are almost spent. And yet we have not much further to go – perhaps now is the time . . ."

So saying, he pulled out of his pocket a small bottle of liquid. It had been given him by a cunning old horseman, who had told him to use it wisely, for though it would give new life and vigour to an ailing horse, making it gallop for as long as it had legs to carry it, in the end, the effort could prove too much. But Dick knew he could not give up now, that he must complete the challenge and reach York, whatever the cost. And he tipped the sticky liquid down Bess's throat.

Its effects were instantaneous. The next moment no-one would have believed that Bess had already galloped throughout the night. Her head was high in the air, her neck proudly arched, her flanks no longer heaving and she was stamping the ground eager to be off.

"He was right," said Dick as he vaulted back into the saddle. He laughed wryly. "I should have left a drop for myself, for I feel near ready to drop too."

But the thrill of the adventure served to revitalize his flagging energy and together they pressed on. As the stronger light of day began to push out the grey dawn, they were almost within sight of York, but once more Bess was clearly losing her strength. Dick had not heard his pursuers for some little while, and wondered whether they had given up the chase, but as they reached the River Ouse, he heard a loud shout behind him. They were hot on his heels after all and the ferry boat he had intended to convey them across the water was still only half-way across. There was no time to wait for it!

He pressed his heels against Bess's flanks urging her down the bank and into the water. Within seconds, they were swimming across. As their pursuers reached the water's edge, one of them urged his horse forward. Not so his colleague, who instead decided to fire a warning shot, not to hit Dick though, for a dead highwayman was worthless, while one who was alive commanded a considerable sum of money.

Skimming across the water, the bullet went wide of its mark as intended, but it had an alarming result, nevertheless. The officer who was swimming his horse across the river gave such a start that he jerked harshly on the reins. The next moment, his horse's head had disappeared beneath the water and the beast began to sink. More concerned now with saving his own skin than catching the runaway highwayman, the officer pulled his horse's head up and the two floundered back to the bank. Dick Turpin and Bess, meanwhile, were scrambling up the bank on the other side.

"Hurray!" shouted Dick. "We must surely get there now, Bess."

Encouraged by the cheery cry from her rider, and refreshed by the cooling water, Bess struck out once more, straining every muscle to convey her master to the safety of York. On she went, Dick leaning forward in the saddle in an effort to help her all he

could, and yet sensing that this was her final effort. And indeed, within sight of the ancient city of York, bathed in the morning sunlight, the lofty spires of the great cathedral towering above them, Bess faltered and fell. For the last time, she looked at her master and friend, through eyes that were now dull and glassy. There was no energy left to give him a last whicker of friendship. With a final deep breath, her eyes closed and her sides were still.

Dick Turpin's triumph of reaching York was forgotten as he rested his head against the lifeless face of his truest and dearest friend, a great lump rising in his throat.

At that moment the cathedral clock chimed seven times. "Oh, Bess, my Bess, how I wish you could have heard those chimes too."

As he sat stroking the mare's head, he felt a hand on his shoulder. Reaching for his pistol, he looked up – into the eyes of a friend.

"Quick," urged the friend. "You must away, before your pursuers find you here."

"But . . . Bess," said Dick. "I can't leave her to them."

"What did she die for, but to save you?" said the man. "I'll bury her for you, don't worry. But now you must hide yourself."

And with one final pat of Bess's head, Dick ran off.

135

Their quarry had escaped. Dick's pursuers found themselves a small inn to have breakfast after their long night's riding. There, seated at a nearby table, was a country fellow dressed in a smock, tucking into a hearty breakfast. "It looks as if that fellow hasn't eaten for a week," said the chief constable gloomily. "Personally, I think my appetite would be better if Dick Turpin were caught and in his place."

The countryman looked up. "What's that you say about Dick Turpin, Master?" he asked.

"Why do you ask?" retorted the constable. "Have you seen him?"

"Not I," said the countryman through a mouthful of food. "But I have heard tell of him. I hear he leads officers such as yourself a pretty chase – covering more ground in a day than you can in a week!" And he chortled as he spoke.

"If that were true, it's not so any more," said the constable. "The fool has just ridden his famous mare to death, by galloping her from London to York in one single night."

"He was a fool indeed to attempt that," said the countryman. "And did you follow him all the way?"

"We did, although he has given us the slip now," was the grudging reply.

"Ah, and how many horses did you use, Master? Half a dozen or so?"

"Half a dozen?" snorted the constable. "Why, we used twenty at least."

And under his breath the countryman said, "Twenty! And I beat you with just one!" Dick turned back to his breakfast. If he had not been a strong, tough highwayman, he might have been excused wiping a tear from his cheek. As it was, his eyes merely glistened.

The Wild One

"LOOK! OH, look over there!"

Cheri, in the lead on the long-striding Pennant, was pointing excitedly.

The others were already looking at the herd of loose ponies wheeling across the forest glade. One – a glowing bay with black points – stood out from the mousy-browns of the rest, and he paused to stare at the riders. A shaft of sunlight filtering through the trees turned him for an instant into a creature of flame. He snorted once, then galloped after the herd.

"Come on!" cried Nick, releasing the eager Eureka's reins.

Despite the long day's trek, horses and ponies were keen to follow the strangers, but in seconds only distant crackling sounds showed which way they had gone.

"Come back," shouted Jan. "We don't want to get lost at this time of day. We've been warned about the bogs here, too."

"Those were wild ponies," said Charles, as they returned to the track. "I'd have liked a closer look."

137

"Particularly at that bay," said Sonia. "He was so beautiful."

"You may see them again," said Jan. "We're staying the night in the forest, and tomorrow we've time to explore a bit."

The night's stand was a small farm cleared from the forest. Mrs Speed had already arrived with the caravan and they were greeted by the welcome smell of cooking. But the ponies had to be fed, watered and turned into a field, the boys' tent put up and the tack cleaned before they sat down to supper. They had just finished when their landlord came over, accompanied by a sunburnt girl.

"This is Mr Crawford and his daughter, Marty." Mrs Speed introduced them. "They can tell you all about the forest."

"That herd of ponies? Are they wild?" asked Charles.

"Indeed," said Mr Crawford. "Scrub ponies, mostly. A few are caught up and used by the local people."

"But there was one beauty, a bay. I'm sure he was no scrub pony," said Cheri.

Father and daughter exchanged looks. "He's known as Wild Fire," said Marty. "He's a cut above the rest."

"We're catching them up tomorrow. Care to help with the round-up?" asked Mr Crawford.

"Yes, please!" Cheri, Charles and Nick answered as one.

138

"Will there be any danger?" asked Mrs Speed, mindful of her charges.

"Not if half of you stick with Marty and the others with her brother, Sam," replied Mr Crawford.

The talk that evening was all of the round-up, but in the end only Cheri, Charles and Nick decided to take part. In the morning they prepared for their adventure, while the others set off for an ordinary ride.

A wiry boy joined the three, riding one of the mousy forest ponies, its mane unbrushed and with burrs in its tail. His saddle was a sack held in place by a strap and his bridle was made of rope.

"Here's Sam." Marty introduced him. She led a pony, similar to Sam's from a shed. This one had a saddle and bridle of sorts but tufts of stuffing stuck out of the padding and the leather had not seen any saddle soap for years.

"Is your father coming?" asked Nick.

"He'll be around in the Land Rover," Sam replied.

Marty jumped astride and led off with Sam, at a trot. Well inside the forest they drew rein. "Your horse looks the fastest, you come with me," Sam told Cheri.

"Nimrod's jolly fast," Charles told him at once.

"And so's Eureka!" echoed Nick.

"The way I'm going they need to be fast as well as handy and not too high," said Marty. "Come on, boys!"

Slightly mollified, the boys followed Marty, plunging into a tunnel of honeysuckle and brambles.

"We spotted the herd half an hour back along by the brook," Sam told Cheri. "If we take the longer way round we can start them off down the valley."

Pennant strode beside the pony, her paces twice as long as his. The forest trees changed to spindly willows and bushes of sallow. Suddenly Sam checked his pony, his hand uplifted. Then Cheri saw the ponies, quietly cropping rushes beside a coiling stream. Wild Fire stood out like a spot of orange lichen among the browns and greens around him.

"We're up-wind of them," Sam whispered. "If we work our way round to that dead tree, we can get them moving the right way."

They reached the tree before the ponies became suspicious, but soon they moved closer together and began to drift back towards

the thicker trees. Wild Fire began to show alarm and quickened them away from the two riders.

"Come on!" Sam clapped his legs against his pony's sides. "Or we'll lose them among the trees."

Pennant flew after him, and Cheri, failing to duck quickly enough, was swept from the saddle by a low branch. Her shout alerted Sam in time to grab Pennant's rein as she tried to dive by him.

"Hop up quick," he shouted at Cheri.

It was an effort for Cheri to mount Pennant even when standing still and it was impossible with the mare revolving in excited circles. Sam jumped off, seized Cheri's left leg and almost threw her up, then vaulted back on his pony and galloped on. Pennant flew after him, with Cheri scrabbling for stirrups and reins as they went. A flash of orange ahead showed they were still in touch with their quarry.

On the other side of the valley, Marty and the boys emerged from the green and scratchy tunnel to where the trees were free of undergrowth.

"They're coming," said Marty. "String out a bit. We must keep

them along the bottom there. It leads into the hollow way."

Then they saw the ponies racing below them with Wild Fire in the lead. Nimrod and Eureka were restless, wanting to go down and join them. Instead, Charles and Nick had to keep cantering parallel, at the same time dodging tree trunks.

"Look out for that boggy patch," shouted Marty, flinging out an arm to point to it.

Eureka dodged the patch of tell-tale bright green, but Nimrod's forelegs sunk in it to his knees and Charles went over his head with a roar. They struggled up, unhurt, but spattered with glistening black mud. There was no time to scrape it off; Charles had to leap back into the saddle straight away to keep with the others.

Meanwhile Jan, Sonia and Clive were ambling along a sandy track when they were overtaken by Mr Crawford in a Land Rover.

"Follow me if you want to see anything," he shouted to them as he went past.

"I suppose he means the round-up. I'd love to see Wild Fire again," said Sonia.

They trotted after the Land Rover, catching up with it when it stopped on a slope overlooking a steep-sided valley.

"They should be coming along down there soon," said Mr Crawford.

"That's the pen we will be driving them into."

Following his finger, they could see some posts and rails where the valley narrowed almost to a walled passage.

"What will you do with the ponies?" asked Jan.

"We only want the bay," replied Mr Crawford. "A dealer's coming for him tonight on his way to the docks. He's making up a load for export."

"You mean Wild Fire is going to be put on a ship, straight from running free in the forest!" exclaimed Sonia. "But won't he be terrified?"

"Very likely," said Mr Crawford without concern. "I'm moving a bit to watch over a place where they could break away."

"How awful," said Jan, as he drove on. "He's only concerned with the money. Not with that poor pony's sufferings, cooped up in a ship's hold, and the probable rough handling at either end."

"I'm sure the others would never have helped if they had known," said Sonia. "What can we do?"

"Stop them entering the pen," suggested Clive.

"Of course!" cried Sonia. "We could stand in the way and turn them up one side or the other. Come on, Jan."

Jan hesitated, feeling torn between the two decisions.

"It's not really our business," she cried. "I believe as a forester, Mr Crawford has a legal right to the ponies. Oh dear, I don't know what to do."

"It's hard for you because you're in charge of us," said Sonia. "You go and join Mr Crawford and leave it to us."

"Yes, you need know nothing about it," urged Clive.

Clive and Sonia started down the steep valley side with no further delay. They reached the bottom to hear whooping shouts and a faint rumbling.

"They're coming!" cried Sonia. "Do we stand right by the pen?"

"The sides may be too steep there for them to climb," replied Clive. "We'd better try to turn them here, where we've come down."

The rumbling of hoofs grew louder and then Wild Fire appeared among the trees. His ears came sharply forward at the sight of the grey pony and chestnut thoroughbred. He checked for an instant and the herd surged round him before they saw what he had seen.

"Whoa, whoa!" shouted Sonia and Clive, flapping their arms.

May Day stood her ground, but Fairy Flag, alarmed by the flapping and the jostling ponies, was not so still. The shouts and the thudding hoofs of the hunters sounded closer on both sides.

Knowing the hollow way led to another part of the forest, but not knowing of the trap, Wild Fire made a bold effort to dash past Clive, and at that moment Sonia succeeded in swinging Fairy Flag sideways.

She towered above Wild Fire, who turned and plunged up the side of the valley, his quarters glistening as the muscles strained under his tawny hide. The ponies scrambled after him.

Marty came galloping into sight.

"They're breaking your way, Sam!" she shouted.

Sam and Cheri arrived at full gallop to see the herd escaping. Some were turned back, but Wild Fire was already over the crest of the hill. The last Clive and Sonia saw of him that day was his long tail waving against the sky like a victory banner.

With Wild Fire escaped, the round-up was abandoned. At first all the riders – except Jan – thought Sonia and Clive had blundered into the way by mistake.

"Fools, dolts!" stormed Sam.

"We were doing fine. How could you be so stupid?" asked Nick.

"Dad'll be mad," said Marty.

Sonia and Clive stayed silent under the storm of abuse. If it was thought to be their mistake, so much the better.

Mr Crawford certainly was furious.

"That stupid pair's cost me good money," he told the Speeds. "Weeks will go by before we can get near those ponies again and we'll miss the boat for good."

The trekkers left under a cloud, but once Clive and Sonia could explain what really happened, they had the rest on their side. Charles, however, was pessimistic.

"You've only put off Wild Fire's fate," he said, gloomily. "They'll have him in the end."

"Yes, they will," agreed Jan. "And he's coming to us. Mum felt the least she could do was to offer to buy him. We'll handle and train him with kindness, and you can all help."

Two of a Kind

JAN CALLED out to the prancing horse as he bucked and snorted around her at the other end of the lunge rein.

"Steady up! Steady there," she cried. Wild Fire, the gleaming bay horse, skidded round on the other end of the rein, nearly pulling Jan over. His one aim seemed to be to get rid of the old breaking saddle.

When he had quietened down a little, Jan drew him towards her, changed her whip and rein over and sent him round the other way. He gave a repeat performance, and her arms ached before he settled into a trot.

"Ready to long rein him now?" called Nick from the rails of the ring. Jan nodded, and he brought a second lunge rein. They were buckling these to either side of the cavesson breaking harness Wild Fire was wearing, when Mrs Speed appeared.

"I'm off to collect Yasmin," she told them. "Any hope of your coming too?"

"Oh, Mum, I've only just started Wild Fire's lesson, and so far he's shown no improvement at all since yesterday!" Jan said, despairingly.

"Very well. But you must spare some time for Yasmin when she's here," Mrs Speed replied. "It's a terrible disappointment for her not to be able to return to her own country for the school holiday as she had expected."

"I only hope she rides and we can entertain her that way," sighed Jan. "Mum knows a mistress at the school where this foreign girl is a boarder and in a weak moment agreed to have her for the holidays," she explained to Nick. "It's a bit of a nuisance when we're so busy."

Jan began to long-rein Wild Fire. It was to teach him to go forward and turn either way in response to her aids on the reins. Sometimes as she tramped behind him, he would go quietly and Jan thought they were making progress. Then suddenly he would do a great leap to one side, or try to bolt forward. Then she would have to let one rein go to its full length and shorten the other to turn him back into a circle.

Today was no better. A rabbit jumping out of a tussock was the excuse for Wild Fire to misbehave and he got a hind leg over one rein. He plunged and kicked nearly bringing himself down before Nick got to his head and Jan was able to disentangle him. She knew if he got loose with the reins trailing he might panic and run blindly

into disaster. Yet he had to be disciplined from the ground before he could be ridden.

Jan was really tired by the time Wild Fire had calmed down enough to be driven into the cattle byre for the last session of the daily lesson. The ground was deeply covered with straw and the byre was small enough to prevent him getting up speed.

"Let me try riding him today," begged Nick.

"Not until he's dependable," Jan shook her head. "He's my responsibility."

While Nick held Wild Fire Jan began as usual by leaning her weight across the saddle. Slowly and gradually she drew her right leg over until she was astride the quivering horse. Although she patted and talked to him all the time, Wild Fire's ears went flat back and his eyes bulged with suspicion. Jan slipped off and on the saddle several times before telling Nick to lead the horse forward. Wild Fire moved a few paces, then bucked. Jan held on to the neck strap, put there for this purpose, as he swivelled his quarters one way and his neck the other. After being dragged along for several strides, Nick had to let go.

Wild Fire plunged on, then stopped abruptly. Gingerly Jan gave him the aids to go forward and he promptly reared with her. Nick

bravely led him on again and then the whole process happened once more. A full hour's work showed no improvement.

"It's as if he resents everything we do," said Jan, wearily, as they paused for a breather.

"I suppose he misses running free with the herd," said Nick. "But he's got company here, and we're as nice to him as he'll let us be."

Just then a toot warned of the car's return. Disappointed at having made no progress, Jan had to turn Wild Fire out in the paddock. He galloped off, kicking out defiantly.

"Yasmin, this is my daughter, Jan." Mrs Speed introduced the guest.

"Hello, Yasmin," smiled Jan. "I hope you will enjoy staying here – do you ride?"

"Naturally I ride. The horses of my country are famous," the dark-eyed girl replied coldly.

"We think ours are pretty good, too," said Jan, trying not to be put off by her manner. "Come and see them when you've settled in."

Yasmin reappeared in smart breeches and boots which made Jan feel scruffy in her working jeans. She inspected the horses and ponies in the stables in silence, then pointed to Banner.

"I will ride him," she said.

"He is young and rather keen," Jan told her, speaking slowly for the benefit of the foreigner.

"All to the good," was the cold reply. "And don't address me as if I were an idiot. I have studied your language since childhood."

They went for a quiet hack round the farm and Jan noted that Yasmin rode competently.

"He needs more schooling," was her only comment about Banner's behaviour.

"I'm aware of that," Jan said. "You'd better ride his mother, Pennant."

"In my country we never ride mares," Yasmin retorted.

On their return, Wild Fire came cavorting up to the rails.

"I will ride that, the bright one, next," said Yasmin.

"Oh, not Wild Fire!" Jan said. "He's not properly broken in yet."

Jan rode on, not wishing to discuss Wild Fire's lack of progress. Yasmin remained for several minutes, studying the fiery horse.

"I will ride him next," she repeated, handing over Banner.

"But I've explained, he's not ready." Jan sounded exasperated. But a blank look came over Yasmin's face, just as if a blind had been drawn down.

Yasmin made no effort to join in the daily life of the Speed Centre. She disapproved of the farm, complaining about the smell of cows and being wakened by tractors. She picked at her food, never offered to help with anything and spent long hours lying on her bed. She refused to ride any of the other horses and criticized the children who came for lessons in tones they were meant to overhear.

"That one will never make a rider," she said, as Jan led round a nervous girl who was clutching on to the pommel.

"Mary has only just started to ride," said Jan angrily, although she knew Yasmin was probably right.

Nick – a competent rider – learned from Yasmin that he lacked finesse and Clive – a gentle, quiet boy – that he was sloppy. And the horses drew scorn, too. Sonia flushed with fury when Yasmin said of her favourite, old Fairy Flag, "At home we would not keep such an old thing alive."

"Far from moping over not going home, Yasmin seems to enjoy upsetting everyone," Jan exploded to her mother.

"If only I'd known what she was like!" sighed Mrs Speed.

What upset Jan most was the interruption to Wild Fire's training.

She could not face being watched by Yasmin while she struggled with him, so training was reduced to brief early morning sessions before the visitor appeared. These were hardly enough to retain what he had learnt, let alone progress any further.

Yasmin spent a lot of time leaning on the rails watching Wild Fire's movements, or, when he was in his box, just standing, staring him in the face. Sometimes Jan thought she was speaking to him, but if she was, she stopped whenever anyone approached.

One day a family came to inspect the Centre with a view to arranging lessons for the son and daughter. As Jan was showing them around, Yasmin lounged up to them and Jan had to introduce her too.

"In my country true riding horses are not kept near the common animals of agriculture," she informed them, haughtily.

"Different countries have different ways." Jan tried to remain unruffled. "We think our horses benefit from being on a farm."

"Tamed, dull beasts, fit only for servants," said Yasmin.

"They don't sound much good here," said the boy.

"Can't we go to those proper stables with the indoor school, Daddy?" asked his sister.

"We'll think it over and let you know," said the father to Jan with some embarrassment. Quickly he shepherded the children towards the car.

"Look what you've done now!" Jan turned on Yasmin, as the car drove off. "Any more of your horrid remarks and you – you can just. . ."

Yasmin gave one of her blank looks, and Jan rushed away indoors frightened of what she might say next. So she did not see Yasmin cross to the tack room and pick up a saddle and bridle. Wild Fire was in his box at the time and it was Cheri who saw Yasmin saddling and bridling him.

"Are you getting Wild Fire ready for Jan? Can I help?" she asked.

"No thank you," was Yasmin's curt reply.

"You've forgotten the cavesson. Jan always lunges him first," Cheri volunteered, unabashed.

Yasmin did not reply, but went on tacking up Wild Fire, murmuring to him in her own language. After sniffing her, he had submitted quietly and Cheri's eyes widened as Yasmin led him from the box.

"Oughtn't you to wait for Jan?" she tried again.

"It is no concern of yours," Yasmin told her shortly.

As she led Wild Fire through a field gate, Cheri thought to herself, "Wild Fire must have come on a lot for Jan to let her school him!"

In the field, Yasmin mounted swiftly and lightly. Used to hours of preliminary ground work, Wild Fire was taken by surprise and stood still, looking bewildered. Yasmin spoke to him again and he walked on hesitantly, every muscle tensed.

Jan, coming out from the house, saw the open box door and Cheri standing by the gate.

"Where's Wild Fire, Cheri?" she asked.

Before Cheri replied she saw for herself! There were Yasmin and Wild Fire moving at an erratic trot across the field.

"Yasmin, get off at once!" Jan cried, in a panic.

If Yasmin heard, she took no notice as she urged Wild Fire forward. Suddenly he let fly. Helpless, Jan saw the gleaming red-brown body bunch up, and spring forward. Lumps of turf spun from his kicking black legs and hoofs as he threw himself about. Yasmin rode out his contortions until he managed to get his head right down; then two sizzling bucks unbalanced her and she hit the ground. Jan started to race across towards her, but Yasmin was on her feet at once.

"Stand back," she ordered. "You upset him."

Strangely, Wild Fire had not dashed off and he let her catch the rein. Jan did not dare interfere while Yasmin remounted, and she watched as the girl caressed Wild Fire's neck, murmuring to him softly. They went round the field – walking, trotting, walking – and although twice the horse's back hunched ominously, it relaxed again immediately at some communication from Yasmin.

"I don't believe it," Jan said to Cheri.

"I told her you always lunged him first," said Cheri righteously.

It was a big field and at times the pair passed from sight, but at last they returned to the gate, Wild Fire walking on a loose rein. Both had the look of those that had come successfully through an ordeal. Wild Fire clinked his bit and moved with confidence and trust. For the first time since her arrival, Yasmin smiled.

"We understand now," she said to Jan. "May I ride him all the time I am here, please?"

"Er- yes, of course," replied Jan, converted not only by Wild Fire's behaviour but by Yasmin's 'please'. Then curiosity forced her to ask, "But what do you both understand?"

"Each other's unhappiness as strangers here," was the almost shy reply. "But now we think perhaps it is not so bad after all."

Brunehilde ~ The Hanoverian

"THIS IS THE LIFE!" Margaret Roberts leaned back on the springy grass and smiled at her cousin, Heather, and her new friend, Eva Landsfeldt. "Just look at that view!" She gazed contentedly at the distant peaks of the Bavarian Alps, the rich green of the woods and hill pastures, and below, in the valley, the little lakeside town with its centrepiece, the *baroque* church of Saint Mary. "All this – and horses, too!"

"But, Margaret," said Eva, in her soft voice, "you have horses at home in New Zealand. What about your own pony?"

"Oh, I know – and don't think I'm being disloyal to my darling Kiri," Margaret replied. "But those marvellous Hanoverians your father breeds, Eva. They're out of this world."

"Well, I like that!" remarked Heather. "And what about Gwyn-ant's ponies – aren't *they* out of this world, too?"

"Oh." Margaret turned quite pink at Heather's affronted tone. "I'm sorry, Heather, I didn't mean . . . it's just that . . ." Then glancing at her cousin's face, she broke off. "Why, you rotter, you're teasing me again!"

"That's right," Heather agreed mischievously. "You're lovely to tease, you fall every time . . . and you're a rotten shot, too," she added as Margaret threw a handful of grass at her – and missed.

Margaret was enjoying every minute of her unexpected Bavarian holiday. When, six weeks ago, she'd arrived from New Zealand to visit her Uncle David and Aunt Nesta at Gwynant, their Welsh Border farm, she'd imagined she'd be spending all her time there – among the ponies. As well as being a well-known show-jumper, David Roberts, together with his wife, was also an acknowledged breeder of Welsh mountain ponies.

"I think they are the most beautiful of all the British ponies," Heather said proudly as she showed her cousin round the family stables, and introduced her to the lively, affectionate little animals.

Then one evening, David Roberts had said, "How would you two girls like a trip to Bavaria? I'm going over to see Franz Landsfeldt, and he's invited you as well – if you'd like to come."

Of course, there was only one answer. Margaret had never been to Bavaria – one of the most picturesque of all the German states, and Heather adored any chance to visit the stud, where Franz Landsfeldt bred the big, brown, handsome Hanoverian horses.

"It'll be marvellous," she told Margaret excitedly. "Dad's known Herr Landsfeldt for ages. They first met show jumping,

when they tied for first place in some big competition and they've been friends ever since. You'll like Eva, too. She's Herr Lands-feldt's daughter – and she knows nearly as much about Hanoverians as he does. Doesn't she, Dad?"

Smiling, David Roberts nodded his head in agreement.

Herr Landsfeldt and his daughter were waiting at Munich airport to greet their guests. Franz Landsfeldt was a genial, grey-haired man, so tall that he towered over the slender, fair-haired Eva.

"How good it is to see you again!" he cried, shaking hands with David Roberts and his daughter both at once. "And this is your niece? Welcome to Bavaria, young *Fraulein*."

If Margaret felt a little shy, it only lasted the journey from the airport to the first intersection of the *autobahn* that led from the bustling city of Munich to the beautiful countryside that surrounded the Landsfeldt stud. By the time the long drive was over, Margaret felt that she had known Eva and her father for years. She soon felt the same about Frau Landsfeldt, who was waiting to welcome them at the doorway of the chalet-style house. It looked so like something out of one of the Grimm's fairytales that Margaret was sure a cuckoo would pop out of one of the little windows at any moment – just like a cuckoo clock.

The following morning, while Herr Landsfeldt and David Roberts disappeared into the stable office to discuss business, Eva and Heather took Margaret round the stables and the paddocks.

"Why do you call it *St. Leonard's*?" the New Zealand girl asked, as they left the tack room with its lines of beautifully polished saddles and bridles.

"Because he is one of the patron saints of horses, and he used to get very angry if ever he saw anyone being cruel to their animals – or overworking them," Eva explained. "In the town of Bad Tolz, in November, they like to honour St. Leonard with a special ride through the streets. Now, come and see my favourite Hanoverian. She's called Brunehilde – we haven't had her very long." And as the three girls walked along the track that wove between the paddocks, she told Margaret about the history of Hanoverian horses.

"Compared with some – like Heather's Welsh mountain ponies – they are not a very old breed. In fact they owe a lot to the Hanoverian kings of England – you know, all those Georges, who used to send English thoroughbreds out here to Germany to improve our stock. On the German side though, Hanoverians are

160

said to be descendants of the war horses of the Middle Ages, and some people say they go back beyond that to Roman times, when there was a Rhineland tribe who were famous, not only for their love of horses, but also for their great riding skill . . . Oh, my goodness." Eva stopped with a little laugh. "I think I am beginning to sound like an encyclopaedia!"

"No you're not," Margaret assured her. "It's fascinating. Tell us about the modern Hanoverians – like your father breeds?"

"Oh, most of them have English blood in them of course," Eva went on. "They are big and powerful as you can see, which means they can be used for both riding and for driving – although most people ride them nowadays. They are very beautiful and very intelligent, and luckily there is a lot of interest in them, so there is no risk of their disappearing and just finishing up as pictures in a horse book. Now, here is my favourite. Brune!" Eva raised her voice and immediately one of the sleek brown horses grazing in the paddock glanced up and came trotting over to thrust a velvety nose into the Bavarian girl's hand. "If you are looking for titbits," Eva laughed, "I have none. Now, behave," she added as the mare rubbed her head playfully against her, "and meet Heather and Margaret. Isn't she lovely?"

Margaret guessed from the way Eva handled her father's horses that she was a good rider, but it was not until she and Heather were getting ready for bed that night, that she learned just how good.

"Dad has been telling me about Eva and Brunehilde," Heather said, as she brushed her hair. "Apparently Brune was considered unrideable when she came here – she linked an accident she had with carrying a rider – and as Herr Landsfeldt told Dad, if it hadn't been for Eva, he'd have been forced to get rid of Brune, but she worked wonders with her. She's too modest to say anything herself, but she really is a *fantastic* rider. Dad thinks she'll make the Olympics eventually."

During the next few days Margaret had plenty of chances to watch Eva riding Brunehilde – and to admire the Bavarian girl's skill and understanding when it came to managing her beautiful mount. Herr Landsfeldt, an expert in dressage, '*high* high-school riding' as David Roberts liked to call it – was only too happy to have both Margaret and Heather join his training sessions. Heather, who had done a little dressage, rode a big Hanoverian called The Grand Turk, while Margaret was given Jason, a bright-eyed, slightly mischievous young gelding.

162

"Don't let him tease you, Margaret," Herr Landsfeldt called. "Use your hands and the pressure of your legs and knees to make him extend his walk as he *knows* he ought! Ah . . . that's right. Now he knows you are determined he is obeying you excellently. Well done!"

Margaret flushed with pleasure at this praise, and drawing Jason to a halt beside The Grand Turk, sat watching Eva and Brune through their paces, almost overcome with admiration. The Bavarian girl and the Hanoverian mare were a perfect partnership. They began *their* exercises by circling the paddock at a collected canter as smooth and flowing as running water, and finished up with sweeping full-pass movement that was as effortless and graceful as any ballerina's solo.

"You know," Margaret murmured to her cousin, "I could sit here and watch Eva and Brune for days."

"So could I," Heather agreed.

During the holiday there was so much to enjoy – the riding lessons, visits to some of Bavaria's castles, churches and museums, and then Margaret's most favourite outings of all, when she, Heather and Eva, went riding through the green woods.

"The best way to see our beautiful countryside is from the back of a horse," Frau Landsfeldt said with a smile, as Margaret helped Eva and her cousin to pack away their picnic, ready for the ride that afternoon.

They set off in beautiful weather – the sunshine and shadow dappling the horses' flanks as they rode through the trees. Eva led the way as they cantered along the wide path, the pine-needles and fallen leaves muffling the thud of hooves. But suddenly, when they had been out for about half an hour, the sun went in, the birds stopped singing and a nasty little wind came sneaking through the trees, making the three girls and their horses shiver.

"Oh, dear." Drawing rein, Eva glanced up at a patch of dull grey sky. "I think we are in for a summer rain storm."

She'd only just finished speaking, when the first raindrops started to fall, slowly at first then faster and faster until they had turned into a torrential downpour. As their horses snorted, pawing the ground and tossing their heads, Eva, Margaret and Heather turned up their collars.

"This way," called Eva, over the noise of the rain on the leaves and branches. "The trees are thicker this way, so we can shelter

better." And at a brisk trot she and Brunehilde led the way to a clump of trees, that were growing so close together they looked like a church porch roofed with leaves and branches.

Thankfully the three girls dismounted, drawing Jason, The Grand Turk and Brune in after them. The Hanoverians shook themselves making their bridles jingle, then, quite used to being caught in the rain, they bunched themselves contentedly together, and waited for the downpour to stop.

"Well, at least it has only been *rain*," remarked Margaret, as the storm began to die away. "Thank goodness we didn't have thunder and lightning too. I don't know about Jason, Turk and Brune, but at home in New Zealand, my Kiri gets very frightened."

"Turk is nervous of storms," Eva told her, "but Jason and Brunehilde take them quite calmly."

As if he understood Jason tossed his head in agreement, but Brunehilde, her huge eyes widening, went suddenly rigid and gave a sharp uncertain whinny.

"Gently, gently." Eva's hand tightened on the mare's bridle as she soothed her. "There's nothing there."

165

"But there *is*," Brune's expression seemed to say, as ears pricked, she stared fixedly at a nearby bush. Catching her uncertainty the other two horses shifted restlessly, while Heather, Eva and Margaret exchanged wary glances.

"I will go and see," said Eva. "Hold Brune, will you please?"

But the mare refused to stay, and although clearly nervous, she insisted on going with the Bavarian girl. A funny high-pitched noise from beneath the bush made everyone jump violently, and for a moment Eva had a job to hold the shying Brunehilde. Then the mystery was solved, as a small, elderly, bedraggled-looking Dachshund crawled out from the undergrowth. He was so unexpected that both Heather and Margaret just had to laugh, while with a cry of 'Goodness, it's Otto,' Eva scooped the wet little dog up into her arms. "This is old Otto," she explained, as the Dachshund, tail wagging, tried to lick her hand. "He belongs to Herr Max Schiller. But where is he, Otto? Has something happened to him?" She put the dog down. "Find him, Otto, find!"

Otto, whimpering faintly, hesitated, then abruptly he hurried off down a narrow path, glancing over his shoulder at the girls and their horses.

"Something *is* wrong," muttered the Bavarian girl. "Herr Schiller, who lives locally, is one of our country's most famous animal painters – but he is old, and also suffers from rheumatism which makes walking difficult for him. He must have had an accident or something in the wood and sent Otto for help – for Otto never, *ever* goes out alone!"

Eva broke into a run as she spoke, and followed by Heather and Margaret and their horses, with Brune pacing beside her, she led the way down the narrow path – to find the grey-haired Herr Schiller in a crumpled heap on a pile of leaves, his walking stick broken in two pieces beside him.

"Hello, Otto, clever little dog." He patted the elderly Dachshund, as he smiled gratefully up at the three girls and their horses. "Eva, my dear, how pleased I am to see you, and your friends . . . As you can see," and his voice shook slightly, "I have had an accident and sprained my ankle. I was foolishly hurrying to avoid the rain, when my stick caught on a stone. It snapped in two, and I fell. I sent Otto for help and I'm so glad he found some. I was beginning to worry a little."

"Well, there is no need to worry any longer," said Eva gently.

166

"We will get you and Otto safely home, never fear. We have three horses, so you can choose your mount."

Struggling to his feet, helped by Eva, Heather and Margaret, the grey-haired artist smiled. "It would be an honour to ride your beautiful Brune," he said stroking the mare's silky neck.

It was not easy helping him into the saddle, but Brune stood quite still until her new rider was settled as comfortably as he could, his injured ankle supported in the stirrup. Then with Eva leading her, and Heather walking beside Herr Schiller, she set off at a smooth even walk. Slightly behind, Margaret followed, leading Jason and The Grand Turk, and carrying the tired little Otto. It was a strange procession that arrived back at St. Leonard's – where Herr Schiller was immediately taken under Frau Landsfeldt's wing.

"Otto and I are so grateful to your daughter and her friends," murmured the old artist as he thankfully drank a cup of steaming coffee, and looked down at his skilfully bandaged ankle. "I must think of a special way of saying thank you."

And he did, too, for when it was at last time for them to leave Bavaria, Margaret had a picture of the bright-eyed Jason and Heather had a picture of The Grand Turk – while in pride of place in Eva's bedroom hung a picture of Brunehilde – three very special portraits painted specially by Herr Max Schiller the artist.

The Winged Horse of the Sky

LONG AGO, on top of a mountain called Mount Helicon, in Greece, the clear, crystal waters of a fountain poured down into a perfectly formed pool close by. It was called the Fountain of Hippocrene and it was here, in the cool of a dewy morning that the great winged horse, Pegasus, would fly down and land as gently as a feather. Then he would fold his huge, golden wings, lower his noble head and take a long drink from the glittering water.

Pegasus lived in the days when Greece was ruled by a great order of gods who made their home on Mount Olympus. He himself, was the child of one of the gods – Poseidon, God of Horses and the Sea. But now Pegasus belonged to the mightiest god of all, Zeus, also known as Jupiter, and it was at Zeus's command that Pegasus had made the spring at the top of Mount Helicon.

It happened during one of the many contests that took place at this time between the people of Greece and the gods. The people of Greece were very powerful and very clever, so much so, that they sometimes forgot that the gods were even more powerful, and also

169

immortal. Zeus had nine daughters, who were the beautiful and talented Goddesses of Song and Poetry, known as the Muses. Their special home was on Mount Helicon, but often they would go to Mount Olympus to sing at the sumptuous feasts of the gods. For the rest of the time they visited the mountains close to where the mortals lived, so they could bestow their special gifts of song and poetry on a few chosen people.

One of the mountains they visited was Mount Pieria which fell within the kingdom of King Pierus. Now King Pierus also had nine daughters and they began to get a little bit too pleased with themselves. Before long they were unwise enough to claim that they were actually the Muses. Zeus's daughters, they said, were impostors. Although Zeus's daughters tried to warn the daughters of King Pierus of the serious consequences that would befall them if they continued to call themselves the Muses, they still persisted. In fact, finally they challenged Zeus's daughters to a contest.

Zeus's daughters were bound to accept such a challenge and during the contest that followed, Calliope, the Muse of Epic Poetry

sang a hauntingly beautiful song, telling of the flowers and trees and fruit and corn that grew so bountifully all over the earth. Of such unrivalled purity and harmony was it that Mount Helicon itself, which had previously been no more than a foothill, began to rise towards the heavens, as if inspired by the magic of the song. From his throne on top of Olympus, where he too was listening entranced to his daughter's singing, Zeus watched the mountain grow higher and higher until he saw it was soon going to be as high as Olympus itself.

"That cannot be!" he cried, and with a click of his fingers he summoned Pegasus to his side. Gently he stroked the horse's flowing mane as he whispered into his silken ears. In an instant the still air above Mount Olympus was broken by a roaring, golden flurry as Pegasus soared off towards Mount Helicon. As he landed on the mountain, he gave one great stamp of his mighty hoofs and the mountain immediately stopped its upward surge of joy. Instead, from its top, the waters of the Fountain of Hippocrene came rushing forth and filled the hollow Pegasus had made with his hoofs.

Pegasus's great act marked the end of Calliope's song too, and there was no question in anyone's mind that she and her sisters were the real Muses. But still King Pierus's daughters refused to give up their claim and so the gods punished them by turning them into a flock of magpies. In their new guise, they fluttered round the

Fountain of Hippocrene, chattering and squawking, just as they had done when they were mortals.

Although Pegasus belonged to Zeus and was therefore constantly at his beck and call, he was tame and friendly to many of the other gods. His particular favourites were Athena, Goddess of Learning, and Eos, Queen of the Dawn. Sometimes they would all meet at the Fountain of Hippocrene as Eos welcomed in the new day. Athena would harness Pegasus with a magic golden bridle and Eos would mount his gleaming white back. Then she would ride out into the sky, just ahead of the fiery sun chariot which was driven by Helios, the Sun God, as he thundered past on his daily journey across the world.

Gods were one thing. Mortals, however, were something quite different and Pegasus did not willingly bestow his favours upon mere men. Only one mortal was ever to become friends with Pegasus. He was a brave young man called Bellerophon.

Bellerophon was a Prince of Corinth, who, after a series of wanderings, came to another part of Greece, called Lycia. Lycia was ruled over by King Iobates and at the time of Bellerophon's arrival, he was extremely worried, for his country was being ravaged by a terrible monster called the Chimaera. This dreadful beast had the head of a lion, the body of a goat and the tail of a serpent. As if that was not bad enough, it constantly breathed great scorching tongues of fire. The Chimaera was ruining King Iobates's country by burning everything in its path and so far it had killed everyone who had tried to stop it.

Now when Bellerophon arrived at King Iobates's palace – a handsome, strong, courageous-looking youth – King Iobates decided to send him on a mission to kill the Chimaera. After all Bellerophon meant nothing to him, so it wouldn't matter as far as

172

he was concerned if events actually happened the other way around, and the Chimaera killed Bellerophon instead. It had to be admitted that this looked more likely!

"If you kill the Chimaera for me," King Iobates told Bellerophon, "you can marry my daughter, Princess Philonoé. Then, when I die you shall become King of Lycia and rule over my country."

"I will try, my king," cried Bellerophon, who had already fallen

in love with King Iobates's beautiful daughter. "But how shall I go about it? My sword will make little impression on such a monster, even supposing I could get close enough to use it!"

"I don't know what advice to give you," said King Iobates, shaking his head. "All I can do is suggest you go and see the wise man, Polyides. If anybody can tell you a way to kill the Chimaera, it will be him. He lives a day's journey from here."

So Bellerophon went to seek advice from Polyides and found him, a gentle, grave-looking man, sitting alone in a hermit's cave.

"There is only one way you can possibly beat the Chimaera," said Polyides when he had listened to Bellerophon's story. "That is to attack it from the air. If you approach it from the ground, you will be burnt up, for it breathes fire all the time, even when asleep."

"But how can I possibly do that?" cried Bellerophon, close to despair. "I can't fly – no man can do that."

"That's true," said Polyides. "What you will have to do is to catch the winged horse, Pegasus, and then ride him to attack the Chimaera."

"But that is just as impossible," retorted Bellerophon. "No man

could catch and ride Pegasus, even supposing he knew where to find him."

"I have a premonition that the gods are ready to help you," said Polyides. "Athena is Pegasus's special friend. Go to her temple and beg her help."

So Bellerophon left the wise man and travelled to Athena's temple, where he fell on his knees and beseeched the goddess's help. Exhausted after his long journey, he lay on the floor of the temple and fell into a deep sleep. In his sleep he dreamed that a gentle and beautiful lady, radiant with the light of wisdom and knowledge, came to him and laid a golden bridle by his side. Then he seemed to hear a voice whispering softly in his ear.

"Go to the Fountain of Hippocrene on Mount Helicon at dawn and lie hidden until Pegasus comes down to drink. Then catch him with this golden bridle and ride him to the Chimaera. You will succeed in your mission, Bellerophon, but beware of mortal pride. Remember you have been favoured by the gods. Without them you would be helpless."

As the voice stopped and the vision of Athena faded, Bellerophon awoke. He sat up and rubbed his eyes.

"Was it just a dream?" he murmured. He looked down at his

side. There lay the golden bridle, and with it, several pieces of lead.

"I wonder what they are for," he thought. Nevertheless he picked them up together with the magic bridle and began his long journey to Mount Helicon.

Across many mountains and rivers and through thick, dark forests, Bellerophon travelled – never stopping for long. At last after several days he arrived one evening at the bubbling, glistening, magical fountain at the top of the mountain. Quite exhausted, he lay down and let the rhythmic splashing of water lull him to sleep, but he awoke before Eos drew back the grey curtains of night to reveal the dawn. Feeling much refreshed and remembering what he had to do, he crouched behind a nearby rock to wait for Pegasus to arrive.

Before long a great breeze all around him and a flurry of wings above told him that the moment had come. With a final flutter of feathers, Pegasus landed lightly by the side of the pool and bent his head down to the clear water. In an instant, Bellerophon had moved swiftly to his side, slipped on the golden bridle and leapt on to the wide, white back.

Pegasus reared up in surprise and soared off into the air, at first trying to rid himself of this mortal who had dared to mount him.

176

Bellerophon cried out, "Pegasus, I am riding you with the Goddess Athena's help, for it was she who gave me the golden bridle. My only wish is to kill the Chimaera so I may return to Lycia and marry the lovely Princess Philonoé. This is why I am riding you, for unless I attack the Chimaera from the air I have no hope of success. Please help me."

Pegasus could sense Bellerophon's mastery. Calmer now, he began to fly strongly and steadily across the sky, leaving Mount Helicon far behind. For Bellerophon, it was a journey of exhilaration, unmatched by anything he had ever experienced before. He felt the power of the beautiful horse surging beneath him, and around him, the air was pure and fresh. Far below, the cities and woods and fertile fields appeared in miniature.

At last they came to a place where the pastures were no longer green and the fields of corn were scorched and charred black.

"We must be over Lycia," Bellerophon said, laying his hand on Pegasus's neck. "Those blackened fields will be the Chimaera's work."

At the sound of his voice and his touch, Pegasus seemed to know

what to do and he began to fly downwards. As they neared the devastated earth, Bellerophon caught sight of a great cloud of flame and smoke billowing out in the middle of one field, and as the fire died away, he could make out the dreadful figure of the monster. He gasped in horror as he viewed its terrible shape. Its savage head was tossing and snarling as the wicked tongues of fire billowed out, and its snake tail whipped this way and that, the deadly, venomous forked tongue never still for an instant.

"Now, fly as close as you can, but keep out of range of the flames or else we'll be burnt to cinders in no time," Bellerophon instructed his magic mount, and seeming to understand, Pegasus swooped down still further, until he was hovering just above the dreadful animal. Taking careful aim, Bellerophon waited until the flames died down for a second, then he threw his spear with all his might, straight at the Chimaera's head. It struck the beast between the eyes, just as Pegasus veered up into the sky once more. Bellerophon looked down expecting to see the monster in its death throes, but not a bit of it! It shook its head as if it had been hit by nothing more than a tiny pebble, and resumed its fiery breathing with renewed

vigour, its strength even greater than it had ever been before.

"What shall I do now?" cried Bellerophon. "If my spear does not even wound it, my arrows will be worse than useless!"

Then he remembered the lumps of lead he had found by the golden bridle and which he had fastened in a bag to his belt.

"Now I realize what Athena meant me to do with them," he said and thrusting one on to the tip of an arrow, he once again turned Pegasus's head in the direction of the Chimaera. As the horse swooped down over the fiery mass, Bellerophon waited for a gap in the flames. Then he shot the arrow straight into the beast's snarling, gaping mouth. Time and again he fitted the pieces of lead on to his arrows and time and again, he turned Pegasus towards the Chimaera. A sea of arrows descended down the monster's throat as horse and man sped backwards and forwards overhead. Now as the monster breathed out its fiery breath, the fire melted the lead and in seconds, finding itself unable to breathe, the stricken beast began to choke. Bellerophon turned Pegasus for the last time, back now in the direction of Mount Helicon, and his last look down showed the Chimaera lying lifeless on the ground.

"We've done it!" shouted Bellerophon ecstatically. "We've killed the Chimaera! Now we can return to Lycia, where I can marry the beautiful Princess Philonoé." And together he and Pegasus sped back through the clear air over Greece.

From that day on, Pegasus never forgot his mortal friend, and often he would swoop down to earth and allow Bellerophon to mount him. Then they would fly off together for a ride of joy and friendship. Sometimes Bellerophon would visit him at the Fountain of Hippocrene when Pegasus descended there to drink. Always, however, Pegasus was first and foremost at the command of Zeus and at night he would fly swiftly across the star-lit sky at Zeus's bidding. That is why you can see him to this day among the stars, shining in the night sky.

A Drastic Remedy

FOR WHAT seemed like the hundredth time, the jet of water from the hose Jan was holding went wide of its mark. "Oh, stand still, Banner!" she implored. "This is supposed to do your leg good."

Banner, the young chestnut horse, was tied to a ring in the wall while Jan tried to hose his swollen foreleg with cold water. It was a tedious performance, and Nick and Cheri, who had been helping to soothe Banner, were just about to go when an old farm worker passed.

"Giving him the cold water treatment are you?" he said.

"Vet's orders, George," Jan replied. "Banner's almost sound after that strain, but his leg is still puffy."

"Sea water, that's what he needs," George told her. "Walking him in the sea for half an hour will do more good than a week of hosing. It always worked with the farm horses in the old days."

"It's an idea," said Jan, turning off the tap. "I'll ask Mum to take us down to the cove in the trailer."

Cheri and Nick begged to go too, and ran off to get their bathing things. Mrs Speed was a bit dubious, however.

"Will you ever get Banner into the sea?" she asked. "After all, it was refusing to jump a small stream that caused the strain in the first place."

"He is shy of jumping water," Jan admitted. "But that's not the same as just walking in the sea."

So the trailer was hitched and they drove down to the sandy cove. It was a quiet place, cut off from a seaside town by a rocky headland. The tide was going out when they arrived, leaving the sand wet and glistening. Jan, bare-footed and wearing her swim suit, led a suspicious Banner towards the water.

As he came within a length of the small waves that splashed into a creamy surf, Banner began to snort in horror.

"Oh come on, boy," said Jan. "It's not deep!"

But Banner didn't seem to believe her. Step into that treacherous, moving water with no sign of land beyond? Not likely! That was far worse than jumping any stream!

Jan turned Banner's head first one way and then the other, trying to get him to move. Cheri, Nick and Mrs Speed made encouraging noises from behind, but he stood resolute. In fact his one nautical achievement seemed to be anchoring himself firmly into the sand.

"Try riding him in," suggested Mrs Speed.

Nick gave Jan a leg up, and digging her bare heels into his sides, she urged him seawards. He took two steps forward. The surf splashed his forefeet and he shot backwards again, before dancing on one spot.

"He's doing a piaffe!" exclaimed Cheri admiringly. "That's dressage."

"I'm not asking him to do dressage," said Jan in exasperation. "And he'll make his leg worse instead of better. Come on, you silly horse!"

When Banner started rearing, Jan decided to give up the struggle.

"You'd better have your bathe while I walk him up and down beside the surf," she told the others. "I might just coax him in at an angle."

While Cheri and Nick waded into the surf and Mrs Speed, who was no swimmer, stretched out in the sun, Jan rode Banner along the shore. The horse's relief was instant. At the shingly base of the headland, Jan turned him back, very gently guiding him nearer to the water's edge. She persuaded him to walk through a shallow, unmoving pool left by the tide, but it was not deep enough to do his leg any good.

Suddenly his head shot up, his ears pricked forward, as he listened. Cheri and Nick, up to their waists in the sea, were yelling and pointing. Following their signals, Jan made out a long red shape, bobbing far out in the water. She trotted along to Mrs Speed, who had jumped up and was also staring out to sea.

"It's a child on one of those air beds," she cried. "He must have drifted out from the town beach."

"With the tide turned, he'll be carried right out to sea!" exclaimed Jan.

"I'll drive to the nearest 'phone and get on to the Emergency Rescue Service," Mrs Speed said over her shoulder as she ran for the Land Rover. Nick and Cheri came splashing over to Jan.

"We heard him yelling for help," panted Nick. "But we can't swim far enough to get right out there."

"There isn't a boat in sight," said Cheri. "He must be terribly frightened."

"Look after Banner while I swim out," said Jan, jumping off his back. "Even if I can't tow the kid in, I can keep him company and see he doesn't fall off before rescue comes."

Jan waded into the water and began to swim. She reckoned herself to be a fairly strong swimmer, but this summer, the riding centre had been so busy, she had had little practice. After some forty strokes she was puffing, but the gap narrowed slowly until she could see the child's white face.

"I'm coming!" she shouted, swallowing a mouthful of water.

He cried out, but she could not hear what he said as she gulped and spluttered. She ploughed on, her legs and arms growing heavier and her chest tighter with each stroke she took. Her eyes were smarting now and she swallowed more water. Suddenly the awful thought came: "Can I make it? And if I do, will the bed hold us both up until help comes?"

Just as her chest felt at bursting point, Jan touched the air bed. The child, a boy of about eight, stopped sobbing, but his joy was momentary, for as Jan clambered across the air bed it started to tilt.

"You're sinking it!" he cried.

Jan let go. It seemed as if her heroism in swimming out could cost both their lives. Then, something in the boy's sudden silence and fixed stare made her turn her head. A dark shape was breasting towards them through the waves. Was it a boat?

No boat, but a dark brown horse with a white star and in a flash,

Jan realized it was Banner, his bright coat darkened by water. There was no mistaking the neigh he gave her.

"Banner, oh, Banner!" she gasped, clutching his mane as he reached her.

Timing it to the swell of a wave, she scrambled astride him. Banner immediately started to turn for the shore and the boy gave a despairing cry. The rein was still round Banner's neck, but Jan could not get him close to the air bed.

In straining towards them, the boy made the air bed tilt so much that he slid off into the sea.

"Swim!" shouted Jan, stretching out an arm and leaning as far towards him as she dared.

The boy floundered, but managed enough strokes for Jan to grip his longish hair and drag him to Banner's shoulders. Another wave helped to push him across the withers in front of her.

Although the boy was small, their combined weight soon told on Banner as he swam towards the shore. He laboured and panted as if at the end of a gruelling race. But the sunlit sandy cove was still a long way off.

"Keep still," Jan said to the boy, who was wriggling about.

She tried to keep her legs clear of the water to make the least resistance, but Banner was sinking lower. Then she heard the hum of an engine above his panting. A launch, throttled down, nosed towards them and a minute later, jersey-clad arms were dragging the riders over the side.

"OK, we've got you!" said a man's voice.

"But my horse!" cried Jan.

"Don't worry, we'll get him back," a bearded sailor assured her.

Edging around, the launch started at its slowest speed for the shore under the control of one sailor, while the second, the bearded one, reached out and caught hold of Banner's rein. Relieved of his double burden, Banner rose higher again and swam alongside with Jan talking to him reassuringly.

Convinced he was now safe, the boy chattered gaily.

"Think I went to sleep," he said, "because suddenly I couldn't see the town any more. I bet Mum will be mad with me for losing the air bed. She bought it new for our holiday."

"I expect that's the least of her worries just now," said the bearded man.

The boat chugged to a halt in the shallow surf. When Banner's hoofs touched the sandy bottom, he staggered for several paces, quite unable to balance properly until he was well clear of the sea.

Cheri and Nick were on the shore to greet them, but most of all they seemed relieved to have Banner safe.

"He would go after you," Nick said. "We couldn't stop him."

"We weren't holding him very tightly," Cheri admitted. "But wasn't he wonderful?"

Wading ashore, Jan, too, felt weak in her legs. She steadied herself with a hand against Banner's shoulder.

"And to think you wouldn't even walk in the surf!" she said as she patted him.

"Well, it's done the trick," said Nick.

"Done what trick?" Cheri asked.

"Taken away the swelling from his leg," Nick laughed. "George was right."

"So it has!" Jan exclaimed. "All the same it's a cure I don't think I'll try again. Next time I'll stick to the hose pipe treatment!"